Mating Lexi

A PLANNED PREGNANCY AGREEMENT EROTIC ROMANCE

APRIL CROSS

TWISTED ROSE
· PUBLISHING ·

CHAPTER

One

"Oh god, Lexi. You're so sexy."

Craig breathes against my stomach. His lips and tongue leave a scorching trail of wetness on my skin. I'm hypersensitive to his touch and shiver whenever his tongue flicks against me. I'm breathless and needy when he gets to my breasts and attaches his mouth to a nipple. Arching my back, I try to force him to suck harder and moan in frustration as he latches on gently. I can't remember the last time I've been this turned on.

I think he might be the one.

Tonight was my second date with Craig. We initially met up for coffee to make sure he wasn't a creep. When I invited him over for dinner, we both knew we'd be in my bed by the end of the night. I have him right where I want him.

He pulls on my nipple with his amazing mouth. When one of his hands slides down my stomach to play with my soft curls, I spread my legs to give him a hint. I'm wet and ready for him. I gasp when he finds my clit, rubbing back and forth at a steady speed. Jesus, this guy is good. I picked a winner this time.

I take advantage of Craig's exposed chest, sliding my hands across every muscle I can reach. He's a swim instructor with an incredible build: tall, lean, and athletic. He claims he's well-endowed. Based on the size of his package in his jeans, I'd say he's a big boy. It looks like Craig won the genetic lottery. Now I just need to get his jeans off him so we're both naked and get that rumored magnificent cock inside me.

I'm edging close to my orgasm, and I want us to come at the same time. I moan, "Oooh, fuck me, please." He stops playing with my nipple and captures my mouth in a deep, toe-curling kiss while he rubs my swollen clit harder.

I grind against his hand. "Do it now. Please fuck me now!"

He hovers over me and rises to kneel between my legs. When I hear the zipper on his jeans, my curiosity gets the better of me. I have to look. He pushes his boxers and jeans down enough to free his cock. It's as massive as he claimed. The tip glistens with pre-cum in the soft lighting, and I lick my lips. Mmm, yummy.

I close my eyes and take a deep breath as I prepare for that glorious first push I love so much. There's nothing like the moment a cock presses into me and my pussy shapes and molds around it.

The crinkle of a condom package wrenches me out of my sexual haze. *Wait, what the fuck?* He said he doesn't like condoms.

I gyrate my hips to tempt him. "Craig, I need you so bad. Just shove it in me."

"Be patient, my eager one." He chuckles. "This will only take a second."

My heart drops to the pit of my stomach. I watch in frustration as he stretches the condom over that beautiful rod of flesh—dashing my dreams with a thin latex sheath. When he presses in, I'm too distracted by my disappointment to enjoy it. Dammit, I guess Craig isn't the one.

When we met for coffee, I'd probed him a bit about safe sex practices and he sheepishly admitted he hates condoms and prefers not to wear one. So why did he feel the need to put one on tonight?

Craig's thrusts become rougher and more frenzied, pounding away at me as his breathing grows ragged. I give the expected responses, and moan and sigh just enough to make him believe I'm loving everything he does, but it's all a charade. I perfected my act over the last six months with all the random hookups in my quest to get pregnant.

After five minutes of him huffing and puffing while he drills into me, I tense my body on purpose and fake cry out with what sounds like an earth-shattering orgasm. I rock against him until he groans that he's coming, twitches several times, and collapses on top of me.

He buries his face in my breast and I hold in a sigh as I caress his hair. Damn it! This month is ruined. My plan to use him all night has gone up in smoke. I was going to send him home tomorrow after break-fast with one last romp to squeeze every bit of nectar from his balls. Ugh.

I track my ovulation and have one window of opportunity each month to find a guy who won't insist on wearing protection. The guys who say they hate condoms and then pull one out during sex are a colossal waste of my efforts.

I narrow my eyes when I hear a soft snore. *Yep, Craig needs to head home.* I buck gently to wake him up.

He stirs and mumbles, "Sorry. I dozed off."

I keep my tone light and flirty. "Hey, sleepyhead. I have an early morning, so I'm going to need to call it a night."

"Oh. Uh, okay."

Craig seems taken aback when I don't ask him to stay, but I'm beyond caring. He rolls off me, and I scoot to the edge of the bed. I throw on a robe while he gets dressed so I can escort him to the front door. Giving him a brief peck on the lip, I pull back when he tries to deepen the kiss. I don't want to be a horrible person by giving him false hope. When he looks over his shoulder and calls out for me to text him, I smile and nod, knowing I'll message him in a couple days and tell him I didn't feel a connection.

Closing the door, I lean against it with slumped shoulders. Fuck. Back to square one tomorrow. For the hundredth time, I wonder if I'm going about this wrong. Maybe I should look for a long-term relation-ship and try having a baby with a partner. The problem is I'm turning thirty-seven in a few months and running out of time. A ball of dread lodges in my stomach. Yeah, this is the best way.

Breakfast the next morning is a somber affair. I pick at my oatmeal and drink a chai latte. What in the fuck am I going to do? It's not supposed to be like this. I never expected to be single and childless at thirty-six. My dream was to have four kids, but I pared the number down the older I got. I'm at the point where having one would make me happy, but the last few years have been really shitty.

Josh, my husband of eleven years, died in a car crash a little over three years ago. We were actively trying to start a family in the months before his accident. Life was bleak for months, and I hadn't been sure there was any point to continuing on. You never really get over losing someone. It took about a year and a half for me to feel anything again.

For a year, I lived on part of the insurance money from the car accident and Josh's life insurance, socking the rest in the bank for a rainy day. Since I'm a pharmacist, finding work isn't difficult, but it's also the reason we waited so long to start a family. I was in school for eight years, and then I had my student loans to pay off. Josh was a tattoo artist, and our plan was he would stay home and I would return to work after maternity leave.

I wander into the living room with my mug and trail my fingers over the wedding pictures on the mantle. God, I look so happy in them. It's like I was a different person. I don't like to think about the dark days, but I'm on the other side of the abyss now and have gotten through the worst of it. I'm a changed person, and I can laugh again and find joy in life. But the desire for a child didn't dissipate because I'm alone.

Deep down, I know I will never be happy if I don't have a child. I had a come-to-Jesus moment on my thirty-sixth birthday when I realized I didn't want another relationship soon. I'm not ready to open myself up to potential hurt, but I still want a child. My insurance doesn't cover fertility treatments, and a consultation with a fertility specialist left me in sticker shock. I want to take several years off if I have a baby without a partner. The amount in my savings account won't stretch to cover that and all those doctor appointments.

So here I am, drinking my latte after another failed attempt at finding my unknowing sperm donor. I have zero plans to involve the guy in any of this, and he will never know. There will be no name under the father's side of the birth certificate. The story I plan to tell my child is it was a crazy night at a party, and I didn't know the guy. I'll weave in details about him being the nicest guy I ever met before explaining I wasn't ready for a relationship and didn't get his info. I'll convince my kid he or she takes after two wonderful people, and I'm sure the guy would have loved to know them.

Is it shitty of me to use a guy for his sperm? Probably, but after many weeks of consideration, this is the direction I'm going with. But having a plan doesn't solve my problem with guys like Craig, who seem like real winners and then pull out a condom. You'd think it would be easier to find some dude to fuck me bareback and leave in the morning, but it's been oddly difficult. It's about 50/50 on whether they forgo protection, but even when they do, of course it doesn't always take. In the last six months, every month I wasn't pregnant broke my heart a little more.

Fucking Craig.

CHAPTER
Two

The people on the dating website I use for my hookups claim they are looking for love, but I only pick people who say they're down for brief encounters. I lied and told my best friend, Kylie, that I was horny and just looking for sex. I didn't mention that I was trying to get the guy's sperm. Kylie laughed and told me to use Tinder so I can swipe left or right, but I don't want to have sex with a bunch of guys. I want to pre-vet them to find out how they feel about condoms first. Hence the coffee dates.

I'm an attractive woman, and I know it. I hate fake modesty, so I won't even pretend I think I'm average. The genetics gods put me in that great category of being cute and approachable, like the girl next door, but I can dress up and look sultry. My long, curly brown hair may be a pain in the ass to style and maintain, but guys love to play with the curls. My big blue eyes and fair skin, along with my curvy body, create a package that's easy on the eyes.

Don't get me wrong, I can be a slob with the best of them. Most weekends I'm in sweats or yoga pants, a t-shirt, and that beautiful curly hair is up in a messy topknot. But for a dating app, I can pick a few cute pictures of myself and get a flood of messages to my inbox. I've gotten good at skimming them and sorting out the guys for the trash can. The message has to hit the sweet spot. Not too short, not too long. If they send me an introductory novel, I'm not reading it, and the same with the one-line guys—no thanks.

Today I have close to twenty "no thanks" guys before I run into one that piques my curiosity. His name is Noah, and his full-body profile picture shows a guy in his forties who would be average if he wasn't so buff in the arms. He obviously lifts weights, but it's not too much. I don't like the guys who look as if they spend every waking minute at the gym. He has brown hair and a yummy five o'clock shadow, but it's the close-up photo of his face that makes my body hum. The most gloriously thick and long lashes I've ever seen on a guy surround his hazel eyes. I'd never want to be fucked from behind with him. I'd want to stare into those eyes all day.

I lean back in the kitchen chair and gawk at the photo some more, imagining those eyes on a kid. Noah must have been the most adorable child ever. I'd pay good money for a permanent solution to get eyelashes like that. I've taken plenty of science classes and I know there's no guarantee with genetics, but for the chance to have a kid with those eyes? Oh, heck yeah.

I flip back to his message. It's the perfect length and has an amusing, flattering tone. I can tell he thinks I'm hot but doesn't want to be creepy about it. The ball is in my court, so I shoot off a flirty reply and compliment him on his eyes. I'm not expecting an immediate response, so I go back to browse the list of new guys to see if anyone's joined in the last few days.

When I get a notification that Noah messaged me again, my stomach flutters and I grin at the screen. Well, well, well, someone isn't playing hard to get, which I appreciate. I don't have the time or energy to chase anyone. I have about three weeks to find a guy who isn't a jerk and screen him on a coffee date to make sure he won't insist on a condom before I seduce him on short notice when my ovulation kit tells me it's go time.

I've been on plenty of coffee dates that were a bust. It takes guts for a man to admit on a first date he doesn't want to use a condom. Since so many guys say they hate condoms and then want to wear one, I'm probably tossing aside guys who would fuck me raw and fill me up. I can't risk spending the time to find out.

Noah and I banter back and forth about stupid things like movie quotes and who is the sexiest actress alive. We agree Sophia Vergara is in the top five, so we already have something in common. When our conversation crosses thirty minutes, I switch to my phone app so I can move around my condo.

Since we're still talking at lunchtime, I use that as an excuse to invite him on what he thinks is a date.

LEXI

> Hey Noah, since we can't seem to stop talking, want to grab a coffee?

My phone app blinks to show he's typing, and he's quick to respond.

NOAH

> I'm down. I know a great café and can be there in an hour.

A rush of excitement zips through me, and I'm breathless.

LEXI

> Sounds good. Send me the info.

I try to temper my eagerness as I get ready to meet him. I've been hopeful dozens of times in the last six months. Chances are he's going to be a dud, but I'm humming as I pick out my sexiest jeans. For good measure, I add a purple V-neck blouse that shows plenty of cleavage. A fantasy runs through my head of being pregnant in six months. It could happen. Maybe Noah is the perfect guy.

The coffee shop is the place around the block from my condo, so I walk instead of driving. Does this mean he lives close by? I get coffee here often, and it's fun to imagine we might have been here at the same time and never noticed each other. Pretty unlikely, though. With those eyes? I'm sure I would have noticed him.

He's not here when I arrive, so I order my caramel mocha and select a corner table. My bad; I didn't time it well. What can I say? I was too nervous and thought I would walk slower. When he's still not here five minutes after the time we agreed to meet, I drum my fingers on the tabletop. Okay, Noah. Anytime now. This isn't looking good for him so far, since I value promptness. But my biological clock is literally ticking, so I should probably be flexible. I check my phone. No messages from him.

My drink is half gone and he's nine minutes late when he finally saunters in. He spots me, smiles, and those gorgeous eyes crinkle at the corners. I try to not let my stony heart melt, but I can't help it. Fuck, who can stay angry at that sexiness?

"Hey, sorry I'm late. I couldn't find my car keys."

Hmm, that doesn't help him as an excuse either, since people who lose everything drive me batty. He's also entirely too casual about being late, not sounding apologetic. I try to tame my inner bitchiness. He's hot, and if he doesn't like condoms, who am I to be picky? I'm not marrying the guy.

I purposely keep my tone neutral. "That's fine. Want to go order your drink?"

"Yeah, be right back."

He leaves the table and stands in line to order, giving me the perfect opportunity to check him out. Everything about his looks makes me tingle. He's tall, fit, and has yummy arms and shoulders. I bet his stomach is flat and has well-defined abs. Usually I don't do a test run with the guy before I ovulate. I got burned once by a guy who only wanted a one-night stand and never called again. I might risk it with Noah. My breasts ache looking at him and I want his mouth on my nipples.

When he returns to the table, he slides into the chair gracefully, sets his coffee down, and folds his hands in front of him.

"Lexi, before we get much further, I should admit something to you."

Uh, oh...here we go.

He takes a drink and continues on. "A few months ago, you dated a friend of mine, Erik."

Erik? Who is Erik? My brain scans through my recent men, but I can't place a face to the name. I don't want to admit I can't remember who that was, so I play along.

"Oh, we didn't work out."

Noah snorts. "That's a bit of an understatement."

As soon as Noah speaks, I realize who Erik was. My stomach clenches in anger when I remember what happened.

"Yeah, well, your buddy Erik tried to grope me under the table on our coffee date without warning, so I poured my drink in his lap."

Noah looks at me seriously. "When he found out I was talking to you today, he wanted me to apologize. He was a jerk, and he's sorry."

I'm pleasantly surprised and relax at Noah's words. That Erik didn't tell him to give me some excuse for the behavior is refreshing. At least he realizes he was an asshole and what he did wasn't okay.

"But Lexi, tell me something...what's the deal with you and condoms?"

Oh, fuck.

Stricken, I look at him and I feel my mouth drop open and my breath catches. What the hell do I say to this?

After a moment I recover, close my mouth, and pretend I didn't just freak out. I have to buy some time while I figure out what I'm going to say.

I fiddle with my coffee cup and try to sound nonchalant. "Uh, what do you mean?"

Noah smiles at me, his hazel eyes twinkling. "Erik said you were fixated on knowing if he liked to wear condoms. He said it was odd for a coffee date."

Okay, so maybe I wasn't so subtle a few months ago. I've learned to be coy about getting the information I need. I still don't know how to respond, so I pull out the class clown routine and go for over-the-top dramatic.

"Obviously, I wanted to milk him for all his sperm and the condom was going to get in the way." I hold my mug in the air and sweep my arm in an exaggerated motion towards my mouth. Luckily, it has a lid and is more than half empty. I take a large mouthful of my mocha and try not to cringe at how stupid I sound.

I wait, expecting a laugh. No one would think I was serious, so he has to laugh...right?

Noah leans back in his chair, definitely not laughing, and studies me with hooded eyes. I can feel myself blush the longer he says nothing. His silence is making this all so much worse.

"You know, Lexi, if that's what you really want, I'm game."

My eyes widen, and I stare at him. Is he really offering me his sperm? Can it be this easy? I shake my head, assuming I'm dreaming, and laugh self-consciously.

"What? Why would I want that? That sounds crazy."

Noah shrugs, leans forward, and takes a sip of his drink before answering. "I was the sperm donor for a lesbian couple who couldn't afford a fertility clinic. They wanted it the old-fashioned way, so I had a pleasant couple of months of banging both of them until one of them got pregnant."

I snicker at him. "You think the lesbian couple wanted to have sex with you?"

I'm trying to change the focus from me, but it's also just like a man to assume that all lesbian women need cock.

"Oh, we all had fun. You know sexuality is a scale. It's not black and white. They don't want to be with a guy long term, but we had a good time trying to get pregnant." He drains his drink and stands up. "I'm going to get another one. Want anything?"

My drink is about empty and I'm not ready to go home yet, but I don't want more caffeine.

"Can you get me a strawberry Italian soda with cream?"

"I'll be right back, and you can give me your answer." He grins at me and heads towards the counter.

Trying to not think about milking him for his sperm, I huff for a few moments about how he schooled me about sexuality. I was the one who was being narrow-minded, but it's never fun when someone calls you out on it. That leads me to considering the whole arrangement. Now that I've met him, I'm not sure I like him. He was fun to chat with online, but he's more of a free spirit than I like. Who fucks two women for a couple of months until one gets pregnant and then walks away? And the lost car keys? No thanks.

He's standing at the counter with his back to me, and I check out his ass. Yeah, he's got a fine ass, and I hum with desire as I imagine running my hands over his tight buns. I wonder if he's ticklish?

Jesus, Lexi, get a hold of yourself. My eyes keep traveling to his ass, and the longer I look at it, the more undecided I become. I've got a hot man who says I can use him for his sperm. Dare I say no? I don't have to like him. I only have to fuck him.

By the time he gets back to the table, I've decided. He sets the drinks down and takes a seat.

I wait until he's comfortable, exhaling a long breath as I say, "I'll take it."

Noah laughs and takes a sip of his fresh drink. "Oh, you can do better than that. Tell me exactly what you want."

What the hell? My nipples harden, and I feel my panties grow damp. I squirm in my seat, hating that him making me say it is turning me on.

"Um, I want your sperm?"

He's got that twinkle back in his eye, but his voice is serious. "Are you sure? You seem uncertain."

Ugh, fuck, this guy is annoying. I snap at him. "Yes, I'm sure!"

"And you want my sperm? How are you going to get it?"

I flush a brighter shade of pink and mumble, "Have sex with you."

"What did you say? Have sex with me?" Noah's voice is louder than it needs to be, and the people at the table next to us glance over and try to hide their smiles.

Now he's pissing me off. "Hey, pipe down. Not everyone needs to know our business!" I'm not sure having a baby with those eyelashes is worth it anymore, but the allure of having a sperm donor on tap has me hooked. Imagine not having to do these stupid first dates anymore? I could call him up when it's time, and he'd come fuck me good.

"Then tell me exactly what you want, Lexi."

Jesus Christ, FINE. I'm even-toned and as clear as I can be. "Noah, I want you to fuck me and get me pregnant."

Saying it out loud and in the middle of a busy coffee shop sends a zing straight to my pussy. I feel myself getting wetter. I almost groan thinking about having sex without worrying about him pulling out or putting on a condom. A man I get to use over and over again and have all his cum inside of me sounds heavenly.

Noah takes a sip of his drink. "Okay, but I have terms."

His statement breaks me out of a cum-filled sexual daze. *Terms?* He better not be about to ask me for money.

"What sort of terms?"

"You're thinking we'd only do this when you're ovulating, right? You're probably tracking?"

I nod at him, and he continues. "I want it twice per week, and then every day when the time is right for you."

Wait, he wants a sex agreement that isn't for baby-making? I laugh at him. "You're that hard up for sex and can't find someone else?" With this guy's looks, I doubt he has problems finding partners.

"Oh, I can have sex whenever I want. You and I are going to get STD tested and then be monogamous until you get pregnant. Neither of us knows where the other has been, and I doubt you've been using protection all the time."

I snort quietly. *Yeah, he's got a point there.*

"I'm not giving up my sex life as a favor for a woman I don't really know so she can get pregnant. This is a win-win for both of us."

Am I really about to barter my body for a baby? I shift in my chair, wishing I was riding his cock right now. Yeah, I think I am. Everything about this conversation is turning me on. Arranging sex like it's a transaction is hitting a kink I didn't know I had, and I'm feeling fabulously slutty right now.

"Lexi, do you agree to my terms?"

I exhale and give my response. "Yes. Let's do this."

Noah holds out his hand for me to shake. When I slide my palm against his, little sparks of electricity flow up my arm and my heart rate speeds up. Something tells me that however long it takes to get pregnant, I'll have fun getting there.

<h1 style="text-align:center">CHAPTER
Three</h1>

After we shake on the deal, Noah studies me. I don't know what his expression means, but I can tell he's contemplating something. I take a sip of my Italian soda while I wait, but I don't have time to swallow before he speaks.

"I think we should do a trial run before we both get our STD tests."

Uh, what is he talking about? I gulp the mouthful of liquid past a tiny cough.

My voice is hesitant when I ask, "What exactly is a trial run to you?"

Noah laughs at me, and I realize he's done it often. I'm about to get snarky and tell him I'm glad I amuse him, but his answer distracts me.

"You know, we have sex as a compatibility test."

My pussy throbs from the mental image of us fucking. I've been vacillating between turned-on and annoyed for the entire date. The thought of sex flips my switch, and I want his cock inside me and his cum dripping out of me.

When I don't immediately respond, he continues on, "Of course, we'd use condoms since you aren't ovulating and we haven't gotten tested yet."

Oh, bleh. My fantasy of all that tasty cum inside of me vanishes, but his point is valid. It would be better to know we're compatible before either of us goes for a test. I try to convince myself I'm being logical and this has nothing to do with how I was thinking of riding him a few minutes ago. It's almost impossible to ignore the tingle running through my body.

I still don't answer, even though I know it's a "Fuck, yes," because I don't want to seem too eager.

I lick my lips, and the movement catches his attention. The glint in his eyes spreads warmth from my chest to my face. I bet I'm bright pink. I didn't mean to make the movement sexual.

To hide my embarrassment, I blurt out, "When do you want to do this?"

He quirks an eyebrow at me, and his confidence almost annoys me. Why do I feel foolish around him? Usually I'm calm and collected, but I keep saying and doing stupid things.

"I was thinking right now."

He's still looking at my lips. I wonder if he's as turned on as I am. I'm half tempted to drag him to the restroom, make him sit on the toilet, and fuck his brains out. But the thought of dirty bathroom sex isn't as appealing as my bed, and it's not like I live far away.

I stand up and grab my purse and Italian soda. "Let's go then."

He doesn't waste time and obediently follows me, tossing his cup in the trash on our way out. I don't mind being the one in charge sexually, and he seems like he's going to be a perfect little toy that I can use over and over again until I milk him dry. It always tickles my fancy when the guys who come across as all confident and cocky end up being my sex slave once I bring them home. So far, Noah is fitting the same mold. Since tonight isn't for procreation, maybe I'll demand he lick my pussy so I can judge how good he is at it.

I pause outside, realizing we didn't discuss going back to my place, but I head in that direction. Glancing over my shoulder to make sure my new toy follows, I state, "I'm assuming my place is fine."

"Yeah, I'm not picky. I can fuck anywhere."

I snort—*yeah, I bet he can.* He's strong enough to hold me up and fuck me. We pass a couple of dark alleyways, and my pussy buzzes when I consider pulling him into one of them. No, I want to be in bed. I want to evaluate his skills, and a quick alley fuck isn't enough time.

When we're almost at my place, I look over my shoulder again and he's studying my ass. A rush of pleasure almost makes me giggle. Well, that's nice. I put an extra swing into my hips as I climb the stairs to the condo building's lobby. As I use the keycode to get us in, he presses his hardness up against my ass. *Well, hello there.* I guess someone is ready for action. My head swims a little, and I put the code in wrong and have to do it a second time.

An intense need for his cock hits me, my hands shaking when I finally open the door. Shit, I need to get him upstairs pronto. I grab a fistful of his shirt and drag him towards the elevator. Normally I'm a stairs girl, to help keep in shape, but tonight I want a few minutes of fun in the elevator.

I live in an old building with a cage-style elevator, and when it arrives at the lobby, I have to push the metal cage open. Noah helps me, and I stumble into the elevator and blindly push the button for my floor. There is an inner and outer cage to keep us safe, and I hear him latch everything closed. Before I know it, I'm shoved up against the elevator wall, face first. I gasp as he grabs my wrists and pins them above my head.

Oh shit, where did this come from? He grinds against my ass, and a gush of wetness leaks from my pussy. *Fuck, this is so hot.* I want him to rip my jeans down, shove his cock into me, and fuck me hard right here.

I'm about to suggest it when he whispers in my ear, "Lexi, do you want me to breed you?"

"Ooooh, yes, please." It comes out as a whimper as I push my ass back against him and shimmy my hips, trying to get more friction.

A cough interrupts us. Fuck, we reached my floor! The outer cage is open and my church-going elderly neighbors are standing on the other side of the inner door. The wave of humiliation at being caught by someone I know heats my core even more. I probably ruined my prospects of any future holiday cookie surprises on my doorstep, but my traitorous pussy doesn't care.

Noah releases my wrists and sounds cheerful. "Oh, sorry. We didn't realize the elevator stopped. Need help with the door?"

He doesn't wait for their answer, and he opens the cage for them.

My face burns red. I can't look at them as they stand aside so we can leave the elevator.

Noah calls out, "Have a nice night," before he grabs my hand and demands, "What's your door number?"

My brain is mush from being turned on and the added dose of humiliation. I stammer out my number, and he pulls me down the corridor. I fumble with my keys. Impatient, he takes them from me to unlock the door. As soon as we're inside, he drops them in a dish next to the door and sweeps me into his arms.

"I'm assuming your bedroom is down the hall." His voice is husky, and I can tell he's as turned on as I am.

I wordlessly point in the general direction of the room, knowing my bedroom door is wide open at the end. My head whirls from the abrupt change. I assumed I was going to domme his ass tonight. Now he's taken control.

I wrap my arms around his shoulders because I want to and not because he's going to drop me. His powerful muscles bunch under my hands as he effortlessly carries me to the bedroom.

Yeah, this is going to be fun.

Noah flips the light on and drops me on the bed. I bounce a little as he grabs my feet and takes my shoes and socks off. Next come my jeans and panties, pulled down my legs together. Shit, he's not wasting any time.

He stops when I'm half naked and removes his shoes and jeans. While he's stripping, he commands, "Take off the rest of your clothes."

I scramble to an upright position so I can remove my blouse and black lace bra. When I'm naked, I watch him finish undressing and almost groan at the sight of his cock.

I wasn't always a cock hungry slut. Since I've been sleeping with multiple partners and trying to get their cum inside me, I've become obsessed with cocks. Noah isn't the longest I've had recently, but he might be the thickest. It's going to be amazing when he stretches and fills me.

When I stop focusing on his cock and look at his balls, I stifle a gasp at how big they are. Holy fuck. They aren't so enormous that they're grotesque, but they look full and heavy. I can't help it and lick my lips, imagining how much cum he must have in there. Fuuuck, this is incredible so far.

Noah pushes my shoulders until I'm lying on my back. He hooks my thighs with his hands and drags me until my ass is on the edge of the bed. I squeal from surprise, and he lifts my feet up to his shoulders. Dang, this is the first time a guy has done any advanced positions right out of the gate with me. Usually we start with one of three positions: missionary, cowgirl, or doggy style. When he rubs the tip of his cock along my soaked slit, I close my eyes and moan. Yeah, Noah isn't like other guys.

He taps his cock against my clit. "Lexi, look at me."

I look at him through my lashes, not wanting to open my eyes fully.

"Do you have any condoms?"

Oh no, do I? He brings a finger to my pussy and caresses my clit while he waits for my answer. I can't think clearly while he's doing that, but I manage a moan. "Check the top drawer of my dresser." I gesture towards it with a hand, hoping I'm pointing in the right direction.

He lowers my feet to the floor, leaving my legs spread. I fight the urge to sit up or close my legs. With the overhead light still on, my position makes me feel vulnerable. When I fuck someone for the first time, I don't usually keep the lights on, and I want to cover up with something. I'm a normal woman and have flaws like everyone else, and I rarely put them on display like this.

The nightstand drawer sticks when he opens it, and I listen to him rummage around for a moment before he says, "Found them."

Oh, thank God. If he couldn't find any, I was going to beg him to ride me bareback. I hear him opening the wrapper. When he moves around to the end of the bed, he picks my legs up and puts my feet by his head again.

"Now, where were we?"

He rubs his cock up and down my slit, and I moan.

"Oh yeah, it was right about here. Don't you agree?"

Why won't he just fuck me already? My pussy was humming at about a five before we got into the elevator, but he ramped her up to a ten. I've never been this desperate for someone's cock this fast.

I whimper, "God, fuck me, please?"

He chuckles and presses the head of his cock against my pussy entrance but doesn't push in.

"If I fuck you tonight, do you promise to be my little breeding fucktoy I get to play with until you're pregnant?"

My breathy, "Yes, I promise," must have been enough because he immediately plunges in, straight to my core.

"Ooooh, fuck!" His meaty cock stretches me out, and my head falls back in ecstasy as my hips instinctively arch to take him in deeper. Tendrils of delight swirl through me as I try to adjust to his thickness. I'm panting from the intense pleasure as every inch of him massages my cave walls.

"Do you like that, my little breeding fucktoy?"

"Yes, God yes." I'm unable to stop myself from bucking against him, trying to force his shaft to move.

"I'll tell you what, Lexi." His tone of voice is almost confessional. "If you beg me to fill your pussy with cum, I'll fuck you so hard your head spins. Deal?"

"Um..." I can't form my thoughts to beg.

"Why don't you think about it and let me know?" He thrusts slowly as an electric current lights me up and makes me crave the roughness he's offering.

Ooooh, fuck—shit. I try to pull myself together, but it's not working.

"Play with your nipples," he growls.

Oh, I can do that. I cup my breasts with my hands and pull at the stiff peaks. He continues his leisurely pace, except now everything is worse. Every time I pinch my nipples, I feel a corresponding pull between my legs. It's driving me wild with need. Pressure builds in my core, but I know I won't come until he fucks me harder.

Noah stops and pulls his cock out.

I cry out, "Nooo!"

He chuckles at me, as if he's in a jolly mood. "I really want to come in that pretty little pussy of yours, but I think I'm distracting you too much."

Ugh, he was making it so I couldn't think, but I didn't want him to stop.

A sharp smack against my swollen pussy lips makes me yelp. A blast of delight zips through me. Holy fuck. What is this guy doing to me?

When he slaps me harder and I get the same thrill, I realize how completely fucked I am. I'm going to do whatever he wants.

"Okay, okay, stop for a moment. Let me think." I attempt to clear my head. Wait, what did he want again? I'm hesitant to admit I forgot. "Uh..."

"Are you're ready to beg me to fill you with my cum?" He brings a finger back to my clit and rubs little circles around it.

Jesus fuck, it's almost as if he doesn't want me to talk. Okay, I can do this.

Catching a moment of clarity, I rush to say, "Please, Noah, fuck me hard and fill me with your cum. Pretty please? I just need your cum. Fill my cunt and breed me. I promise I'll be the best fucktoy you've ever had, please?"

He caresses my clit harder.

I whimper, "Please, Noah. I need your cum."

When he stops rubbing, and I feel the tip of his cock nudge against my cave entrance, I almost purr from the pleasure. I cut myself off in case it makes him stop what he's doing. He presses in with one long stroke, nestling in until he bottoms out, while waves of bliss wash over me.

"Yes, my little fucktoy. I'll give you my cum," he announces and pulls out, only to slam back into me.

"Ooooh, my god!" I gasp out as he fucks me ruthlessly. My moans mix with the squeaking of the bed. I continue to play with my tits, loving how it's increasing my pleasure.

I barely get over one ping of ecstasy and he's thrusting in again and another one hits me. I'm quickly spiraling towards my orgasm, and he moans whenever he sinks into me.

"Such a...good...little...breedable...fucktoy." He whacks against me, groaning with every word.

When he brushes a finger against my clit, I slip over the edge. I scream, "Oh, god yes!" as I come all over his cock. I writhe against him as he roars that he's coming, and waves of rapture surge from my core, traveling through my entire body.

He drills into me for a moment longer, and the intense aftershocks of delight are almost too much for me. I quiver with each thrust. When he finally pulls out, the room swirls around me and I let out a tiny giggle. He promised to fuck me hard enough to make it spin.

I'm not able to speak coherently and instead give a faint, "Umph."

My eyes are closed, and I barely notice when he lowers my legs and tugs me up onto the bed so my head is on a pillow. After a moment, the bed dips and he lies next to me, pulling me into him and forcing me on my side so I'm the little spoon.

The room smells of sweat and sex, an intoxicating scent that lingers in the air as a reminder of the pleasure. A film of perspiration clings to our skin, giving us a subtle sheen, and makes me feel more connected to him. His quiet presence is soothing and comforting as I float in my happy place for a few minutes. This is the good stuff.

After what feels like ten minutes at most, Noah climbs out of bed. "I need to get going. Do you want any water or a snack?"

I blink at him. Wait, what? He's leaving? I like more cuddles than this, but I won't ask for it. I don't know him well enough, and I'm a limp noodle that can barely think.

"No, I'm fine. Just lock the door on the way out." I lie about wanting food, even though I could use something, as well as a cold beverage, but I don't let my voice betray how I really feel. If he wants to go, he needs to get out of here before I say something I regret, like begging him to snuggle longer.

He walks over to the side of the bed and kisses my forehead.

"Thank you for the wonderful time, Lexi. I think this is going to work out. Don't you?"

Despite my misgivings, he rocked my world, so I smile weakly at him. "Yes, I think it will."

After he leaves, I lie in bed and daydream about the amazing sex. Fuck, where has he been all this time? Even without snuggling with me as long as I wanted, I'm already craving him again. The throb between my legs reminds me someone hasn't pounded me this hard in a while, and I giggle. If I had known it was going to be this good, I would have skipped the awkward coffee date and told him to get his ass over here.

Knowing I really need sustenance, I drag myself out of bed, pausing long enough to put on my pink terrycloth robe. I shuffle to the kitchen and wince at a twinge from between my legs. I hope I'm not too sore tomorrow. It's probably a good thing I'm not pregnant yet.

I pull open the fridge and survey the contents. Is fucking that hard okay when you're pregnant? Not that it matters. Once I'm pregnant, Noah won't be fucking me anyway. I grab a yogurt and pre-packed meat and cheese rolls, and smile softly to myself. This arrangement started off with a bang. Fucking him twice a week won't be a hardship, that's for dang sure.

CHAPTER

Four

I'm a little sore the next morning, but not enough for a painkiller. Humming as I make coffee, I'm still relaxed from the intense orgasm. I keep expecting Noah to message me. We agreed to sex twice weekly, so we need to discuss if this is going to be scheduled or if he's going to come over whenever he wants and fuck me.

I pause as I'm about to add creamer to my cup. The thought of him coming over whenever he wants clouds my mind. He could bend me over the nearest surface and pound away until he shoots his load into me. I wouldn't even need to come. He could immediately leave and all that delicious cum would drip out of me long after he's gone.

Well fuck, that's a hot daydream. To have any chance of fast and dirty sex, I need the STD test. A quick internet search provides the closest woman's clinic that offers testing, and I make an appointment for tomorrow.

I putter around the rest of the day, keeping my phone on me for the eventual message from Noah. I get a message from Kylie, but I don't want to tell her what's going on, so I let her know I'll talk to her in a couple of days. The longer I don't hear from Noah, the grumpier I get. When he hasn't contacted me by bedtime, I'm miffed. Who fucks someone like that and then doesn't contact them the next day?

I sleep until it's almost time for my appointment in the morning, and he still hasn't messaged me. I grumble as I get ready and grouse internally the entire time at the clinic. Even sitting in the waiting room, I can't get it out of my head while a kind-looking elderly woman in the chair next to me chats about the weather.

When the conversation lulls, I ask her. "Why would a guy have amazing sex with someone and then not contact them for over a day?"

As soon as the question leaves my mouth, I know I sound like an idiot. Noah's got me so wound up I'm asking strangers about his motives.

The lady looks at me with wise eyes, pats my hand, and says, "Because some men are idiots, darling."

I huff, "Yeah, he's dumb," and drop the conversation.

A nurse calls out the older woman's name. As she stands up, she gives me some advice. "Don't worry about him. He'll be calling you."

I thank her, and watch her amble over to the nurse. She's wrong in one detail. Noah doesn't have my phone number and can't call me. All his messages come through the dating app. But she's probably right overall. He's going to want sex again within a few days. He'll be in contact.

I'm in and out of the clinic fast, eager to let Noah know I took my test. I try to keep myself occupied by cleaning while I wait. Regrettably, it doesn't take long since I'm fairly good at straightening up after myself. My condo has a simple layout with a living room, dining room, kitchen, and two bedrooms. Even the two bathrooms are quick to clean, since I mostly use the one attached to the master bedroom. My day drags with zero activity from my phone.

I turn the app notifications off when I go to bed without hearing from Noah. Clutching an old stuffed teddy bear in my arms, I cuddle against it and wish I didn't feel so insecure. I don't even want a relationship with him, so why is this bugging me so much? He's just my willing sperm donor, so I need to get over the bit of hurt from him not immediately calling me and reaffirming how wonderful of a night it was.

Maybe it wasn't that amazing for him?

The thought doesn't help me sleep, and it's a long time before I drift off.

~

When I wake up the next morning, I immediately reach for my phone to check if Noah messaged me, but I stop my hand before I pick it up. I have notifications turned off, so I would have to click into the app to see if he sent me a note.

You know what? Fuck this shit. I'm acting like an obsessed girl-friend, and that's not me. He'll message when he wants to. If he hasn't in a couple of days, maybe then I'll message him.

Dragging myself out of bed, I take my phone to the kitchen with me but purposely set it screen side down on the counter to avoid the temp-tation to check the app. I fill my electric kettle and wait for it to heat.

I'm tense and my day has barely started, so I decide to meditate after I get some caffeine in me. I munch on a breakfast bar—I'm too distracted to bother cooking anything—and I let my green tea steep while I finish eating. Taking my mug with me, I head to my living room to meditate. I work the mid-shift today and have several hours to kill until work. I should be able to calm myself before then.

I settle on the floor in a comfortable position, set my mug next to me, and look at my phone. I'm so tempted to check for messages. My finger hovers over the icon for a few seconds before I press the medita-tion app instead. Selecting the next lesson in the series I'm doing, I close my eyes and try to relax while a guy with a soothing voice walks me through a guided meditation.

After the fifteen minute session, my mind is more settled and I can breathe easier. Something about Noah gets me worked up. My gut instinct in the coffee shop was probably correct. Do I want to be with a guy who loses his car keys and is late to a date? This probably is a bad idea.

I take a sip of my tea and glance at the screen of my phone again. If Noah is a no, then I need to get back on the wagon and find another guy before I'm ovulating. I sigh at the thought of another coffee date. Maybe I need to be less picky with the next guy. And why did Noah have to be so good in bed? Dammit, he should have contacted me. I open the app with renewed determination and hit enter on the login screen.

When the page pulls up, I'm immediately notified that I have a message from Noah. My mouth goes dry and my heart races while I stare at the notification. I open it and the time stamp shows he sent it shortly after I went to bed last night. Well, shit. This is what I get for being Miss Cranky Pants all morning.

He leaves his cell number, and a fluttery sensation in my stomach kicks in when I consider texting him. I re-read the note while absently caressing my neck. The second time I read, "we'll be seeing a lot of each other," a tingle spreads through my body and I feel myself growing wet as I think about how amazing the other night was.

I giggle before turning my phone screen off, getting up, and taking my tea to the kitchen. A few minutes ago, I was determined to date other guys, and now all I can think about is fucking Noah again. I copy and paste his number into my phone's contacts while justifying what I'm doing. Sticking with him is for the best, since I want to get pregnant ASAP. Everything will be fine once we discuss a schedule. I won't expect him to text me on off days, and I can stop obsessing.

I lean against the counter, and a twinge between my legs makes me want to go back to bed and play with my favorite sex toy. Instead, I punch in Noah's phone number and shoot him a quick hello, letting him know that texting works fine for me. After I hit send, I slip a hand down the front of my pajama pants and under my panties. I'm soaking wet, and I moan as I slide my fingers against my clit. I check the time on my phone. It's still over two hours before I have to leave for work. Since I don't know how long it will take Noah to reply, I might as well spend some time in bed having fun.

I leave my mug in the kitchen. In the bedroom I pull out my favorite dildo and a vibrating egg I like to press against my clit. I don't think I'm going to need any lube, but I take the bottle just in case. Fluffing my pillows, I ready my bed and set the toys on the nightstand. Usually I watch porn or read erotica, but the ache between my legs tells me I don't need any of that today. I'll just close my eyes and imagine Noah fucking me.

I quickly strip, climb into bed, and contemplate the toys. Do I want to warm up with the vibrating egg first?

Yes. I turn it on a low setting and slide it between my slick folds. The gentle vibrations have me moaning within a minute. With the two-toy combo, it never takes me long to orgasm once I'm warmed up enough to turn the vibrations up to high speed. I think about the night with Noah and how dominating he was as I move the egg in a circular motion against my clit. God, this is just what I needed this morning. Pings of pleasure rush through me, and I'm going to imagine Noah as I slide the dildo in.

Since becoming a widow, my sexual journey has been eye-opening, but no one has ever forced me to beg during sex before. It was hotter than I expected, and calling me a breeding fucktoy? That only amplified my frenzy. My husband was sensual and romantic. He'd set candles around the room and make love to me for hours, but I'd rarely call it fucking. With Noah, I felt fucked.

It was amazing.

Despite all my grousing, deep down I'm thrilled Noah contacted me and that I didn't look for other guys to date. Noah might have some annoying traits, but he's willing to be a sperm donor. Having sex with him twice a week is going to be more sex than I've had in years. He could fuck me exactly like he did before, every single time, and I would love it.

My pussy clenches at the thought of his cock, and I reach for the dildo. Right before I slide it in, I turn up the vibrations on the egg toy. As I press the plastic shaft into my wet cave, my toes curl from the ripples of bliss created by the two toys. Mmm, this is so good.

I spear the dildo in and out, and pressure mounts in my core while I imagine Noah fucking me. He's been the first truly great sexual experience I've had in the last six months, and it's nice to have someone to fantasize about.

Everything about it rocked my world. I'm not an exhibitionist, so wanting him to fuck me in the elevator is not something I'd normally think about. He brings out the wild side of me. What more could I want from a fuck buddy? Wishing he was here now, I thrust the toy inside me harder as I edge closer to my orgasm.

Even when no one is with me, I'm not quiet when I touch myself. My moans and gasps fill the room. I close my eyes and, other than having to move the toy myself, it really feels like Noah is fucking me. Pressing my feet against the mattress, I tilt my hips to get a different angle with the dildo, and the new position spirals me over the edge.

I cry out as waves of ecstasy crash into me, and I quiver as my muscles clench and spasm against the toy. I can't think of anything but Noah and imagine it's his thick cock causing all this pleasure as I ride my orgasm.

When I finally come down, I giggle. Dang, that was a good one. My solo play usually isn't a powerful orgasm, but having someone to daydream about amplified it.

Switching the egg off, I remove both toys and set them on the bed beside me before snuggling under the covers with my head on my pillow. My body is relaxed, and I'm drained of any desire to get up. I'm drifting in a blissful haze, and I need a few minutes to recover. I wonder what Noah is doing right now.

My phone dings, announcing a text message. I get an immediate jolt of excitement. Is it Noah? A quick glance at the lock screen shows it's him, and my hands shake as I swipe at the screen. It's stupid to get this excited. I'm sure it was the orgasm. It put me in a heightened emotional state. That's the only reason for the shaking. Yep, the only reason.

I take a deep breath and read the message.

NOAH

> Hey, Lexi. Thanks for the text. I think this will be better than the app.

Hmm, I was hoping for a more interesting message. He was so funny and sweet that first day we talked on the app. I want to flirt a little and not have this be a dry text exchange. Damn. My brain is fuzzy from the orgasm and I can't think of anything sexy to respond with. Oooh, wait, maybe I can!

LEXI

Hey. I was just thinking about you.

I wait for him to take the bait and laugh when he does.

NOAH

You were? Only good thoughts, I hope.

Yeah, this is more like the flirting I was hoping for.

LEXI

I'm lying in bed and they were VERY good
thoughts.

The sexual zing I get from teasing him wakes my brain up, and the fuzziness recedes. I smile evilly when I add.

LEXI

It's really a shame you weren't here to watch
what I was doing while thinking about you.

When he doesn't respond immediately, a stab of disappointment hits me. Dang, just when it was getting good. I watch the clock on my phone for a minute. Just when I'm about to set it down, he finally messages me.

NOAH

Okay, I'm intrigued and now I'm lying in my
bed too. Maybe you should explain this
better so I can get a good visual.

Someone wants to sext with me! I'm getting a nice tingle from the banter, but I've had my orgasm. He might need some punishment for taking two days to message me.

LEXI

Oh, do you think you're a good boy and
deserve to know?

I snicker at his next response.

NOAH

> I'm always a good boy, and I got my STD test. I deserve a treat for that.

Hrm, should I give him a treat? Since I don't know him well enough yet, I'm not sure which is the best way to go. I'm going to have to just go with my gut feeling.

LEXI

> No, getting the test gets you a treat the next time you come over to fuck me. Speaking of, when will that be?

The little indicator bubbles light up for a long time. He's either writing and re-writing his response or typing out an epic paragraph.

NOAH

> I'll get my test results in 3-4 days. If you haven't done your test yet, maybe we need a second trial run? That first one wasn't enough data to tell if we were compatible. This is going to take multiple sessions.

I laugh aloud at his message. Dang, he's adorable when he's not annoying me. I quickly type back.

LEXI

> I took my test yesterday, so I'll have my results before you. We should wait and do a proper second run once the results are in.

His reply is a cute grumble with him agreeing to wait. I tell him I have to go but hint that later tonight or tomorrow I'd describe what I was doing while I thought of him. His "I look forward to it" message has me smiling as I set down the phone. I'm pleased with myself and how I handled the conversation. We definitely have the sexual chemistry part down.

I get out of bed, clean my toys, and put them away. With Noah around, maybe I'll be using them less. The stress from this morning melted away after my meditation, orgasm, and the fun banter with Noah. I hop in the shower, making sure I'll have time to make lunch to take with me.

As I shampoo my hair, I eye the bench in my shower. I'm so going to drag Noah in here with me one of these nights. I haven't had shower sex in over three years, and I miss the freshly fucked yet clean feeling you have afterwards.

After I prepare my finger food lunch, I finish getting ready for work. As I head out the door, I realize that Noah and I didn't share many personal details. I wonder what he does for a living? I also never asked him where he lived. He said it was close to the coffee shop, but we live in an area with tons of houses and apartments, so it could be anywhere.

I shrug aside the thought and decide to weasel more information out of him next time we talk. I can offer him "rewards" in exchange for information. Would a picture of my boobs be worth his occupation? My pussy gets wet at the thought of all the ways I can play with him. Yeah, this is going to be fun.

CHAPTER

Five

We spend the next two days exchanging text messages constantly. When I wake on the third day, the first thing I do is check my phone to see if he messaged me. So far, his morning texts are always cute, and my heart rate speeds up when I see the indicator dot that I have a message. This time there is an animated GIF of a cartoon bear holding out a cup of tea for me to take. I hadn't told him my preference for tea in the morning, and I'm pleasantly surprised it wasn't a mug of coffee.

I'm determined to learn more about him. Twice weekly fuck sessions warrant knowing details, right? He could have some important-to-know skeletons in the closet that I need to be aware of. I'm also curious if we'll ever fuck at his place, rather than at my condo. It would be nice to see where he lives and considers home. I don't know how much of personality is predetermined by nature or developed by nurture. I figure there's no harm in investigating his lifestyle, since my child might take after him.

I climb out of bed and get ready for work. Normally today is a day off, but I'm doing a half shift for another pharmacist who is going through chemo treatments. We're all pitching in to help fill the schedule when she needs time off.

The pharmacy is busy and the four hours speed past. Before I know it, I'm home and in my pajama pants, lounging on my couch. It's only 2 p.m. but fuck it, I'll wear pajamas all day if I want to. My husband used to tease me when I wore sleepwear during the day, and I can still hear his laugh in my head.

The pierce to my heart whenever I remember little things about Josh gets fainter as time passes, but I don't think it will ever disappear. I'm just thankful that I can remember the fun times with him and smile instead of breaking down. This is also why Noah feels safe to me. I'm not trying to have a relationship with him, so I don't have any guilt that I'm looking for Josh's replacement.

I snuggle into the cushions, and my phone trills with a text message. I assume it's Noah and my heart leaps into my throat, but it's the clinic sending my test results. Everything came back clear, so I take a screenshot and giggle as I compose a message. Now I can really tease him, since I'm ready to fuck without a condom, but he isn't.

LEXI

Hey, I got my results back. I'm all clear. You ready to come fuck me yet?

It doesn't take long for him to reply.

NOAH

I can be there in 15 minutes.

I can't hold in the bubble of laughter at his impatience. Since he should have his results in a day or two, I'm going to make him wait for sex. The next time he comes inside me, I want the naughty sensation of his cum dripping out of me afterwards. A zing of desire shoots through me as I imagine how it's going to feel, and I reach my hand down and rub my pussy through the fabric of my pajamas and panties.

My fingers dancing over my pussy gives me an instant rush of pleasure, tempting me to forget about sending him a message. I reluctantly remove my hand, sighing in resignation, and type out a text letting him know I don't want him coming over.

LEXI

Remember, no treat for you until your test results come back.

He does a cute grumble about being a good boy and still getting no treats, and I decide to give him a little something. Pulling my shirt up above my tits, I snap a selfie of them, careful to crop my face out. I send it to him with a little smiley face emoji. His immediate reply to me doesn't disappoint.

NOAH

You're killing me here. You sure you don't need company?

I get a lift from the power trip of having control, and my aching pussy almost convinces me to say yes, but I hold firm. I text him a simple...

LEXI

Nope!

Curious about what he's going to say, I move my hand down to rub myself through the fabric while I wait for his next plea. I desperately want to slip my hand underneath my panties and finger fuck myself while daydreaming of him. I also like the anticipation of holding out until I see him again. The more we flirt, the harder it becomes to wait.

His next message makes me sit straight up.

NOAH

Okay. I'll just sit here and rub my cock without you.

Oh, hell no! I'm not going to edge myself if he's not.

I wonder what would happen if I called him. Would he want more than sexting? Butterflies flutter in my stomach, but I take a deep breath and call. It rings twice before he picks up.

His voice is husky when he answers. "Hello, Lexi."

As soon as he says hello, I want to hang up and toss the phone across the room. My gut churns, and I'm dizzy. Oh my God, why did I call him? I need to stop acting on my impulses. I'm struck silent and don't respond.

After a moment, he speaks again. "I know you're there. Do you want to know what I'm doing right now?"

Some of the tension drains from me. Oh, he knows why I called.

"Yes," I breathe out softly and slip my hand underneath my panties.

I almost groan from the pleasure of my finger brushing against my clit but hold it in. I don't want him to know what I'm doing, though it seems a little silly since I called him up for this exact reason.

"Okay. I want you to touch yourself at the same time and imagine me across the room, watching you and stroking my cock. Can you do that for me?"

A pulse of electricity runs through my core at his words. Oh, fuck. He's good at this. I peep out a small, "Yes," and imagine him across the room sitting on the raised brick hearth of my fireplace, stroking and watching me. Thinking of him here in the room with me but not touching me is erotic, and a gush of wetness leaks from my pussy. I get my fingers slick from the extra lubrication and rub circles around my clit. I moan loudly, and this time I don't hide it. He groans in response and the hitch in his breathing tells me he's enjoying himself.

We play with ourselves for a few minutes, getting louder with our moaning as the other one increases the volume. I can't believe how hot it is to be on the phone with someone while they're touching themselves at the same time. I close my eyes as I press a digit into my pussy, getting lost in the sensation.

"Lexi, what would you want me to do to you if I were there right now?"

My mind whirls at his question. Why does he insist on making me think when all I want to do is bliss out from the intense pleasure? I open my eyes and glance around my living room, hoping for inspiration. My living room is pretty standard: a plush gray microfiber couch, a matching love seat, the fireplace, TV, and coffee table. The empty patch of carpet in front of the fireplace gives me an idea.

"I'd want you to fuck me from behind while I'm on my hands and knees in front of the fireplace."

He doesn't reply, but his breathing picks up and I can hear the faint noise of him stroking. Well, fuck, that's hot. I lean against the armrest of the couch and spread my knees wider, focusing on finger fucking myself. When I slide in a second digit so I can imagine the extra fullness is his cock, my toes curl against the cushions and I'm edging towards my orgasm. I picture him behind me, a firm grip at my waist as he pounds my pussy.

When Noah groans extra loud, I almost come. I'm hovering at the peak and know I'll tumble into my orgasm any second. I'm ready to let myself go when he interrupts me.

"Okay, now stop touching yourself."

Whaaaat? Just him saying that breaks my concentration, and my climax recedes. I stop moving my hand. What the fuck?

I'm at a loss for words. "Uh...."

He gives a soft chuckle. "Did you stop?"

"Yes." My voice sounds tiny and confused to my ears and mimics how I'm feeling.

"Good. Neither of us gets to come until I'm inside you. Agreed?"

Jesus Christ. Can I take back what I thought earlier about enjoying the anticipation? I'm mentally fuzzy and trying to understand what's going on.

I'm hesitant, but I ask, "Why?"

His voice is soothing when he tries to explain. "This will make our orgasm together even better. Trust me."

Fuck, how did I end up with a guy with self-control? I sigh sadly and remove my hand from my panties, wiping it dry on my pajamas.

I can't hide my sullen tone. "I suppose."

I'm not sure how this went from me denying him a treat to him edging me, but then I remember what happened in the coffee shop. I assumed I was taking him home to turn him into *MY* fucktoy, when instead he turned me into his. A blast of heat floods my core as I think about the other night when I agreed to be his breeding fucktoy. I'm tempted to touch myself when we get off the phone. How will he know anyway?

As if he was reading my thoughts, he responds. "Don't think you can get away with playing with yourself. When I get my test results, I'm going to fuck you so hard you'll confess to anything as long as I let you come."

My brain blips out at his words, and a deep yearning hits me. He's right. If I touch myself and he asks whether I did, I'll rat myself out. A snide part of my brain pipes up and asks me what he's going to do about it.

I snort at the notion and ask, "What will happen if I play with myself?"

His voice is hard. "Then I'll fuck you until I come and stop before you get there."

A thrill shoots through me. I let out an "Umph" in a whoosh of air. The tone of his voice tells me he really would do it.

Dang, Noah plays hardball.

Noah decides we both need to calm down and changes the subject. We chat about our day. He mentions he owns a cat named Bandit, and I get a pang of sadness for my last pet. My elderly cat, Sammy, died shortly after my husband did. It was a shitty time in my life. I planned on getting another pet once I dug myself out of my hole of grief, but once I started thinking about a baby, I waited. So I don't tell him about my Sammy and just mention I love cats.

Since he's revealing a little about this life, I'm hoping he'll tell me where he works. I ease into it by talking about my job, the coworker who is going through chemo, and how it was my day off but I covered a shift for her. He's abnormally quiet after I tell him, and I worry it was too heavy a topic. This isn't a "real" relationship, so it's difficult to know how much he wants to know about me. If he's the type who likes to keep things light and playful, I probably shouldn't tell him about the sad parts of my life.

I'm about to apologize when he says, "I was married before."

Oh, yay! He's offering info without me having to pry. I keep my voice casual.

"Oh?" I'm rewarded when he continues.

"We married young. I was 22. Didn't have kids. She passed away when I was 32. Not something I talk about often."

Oh, fuck. My hands shake while my chest tightens and a heaviness settles in my gut. Time slows down while I struggle with how to respond and tears prick my eyes. It's stupid how, even now, I don't know what to say to someone who mentions a loss. The first thing I learned after my husband died is how annoying general platitudes are. Don't tell me he's in a better place, or that it was God's will, or that I'll see him again someday. I had so many people tell me he was in a better place that after a while I got furious every time someone said it. A simple, "I'm sorry for your loss," is best all around. If Noah's in his 40s, this was over ten years ago. Telling him, "Sorry for your loss," isn't the right response.

He also gave me the perfect lead-in to tell him about Josh, but I'm not prepared. I assumed we'd get to know each other for weeks before I casually mentioned my husband in conversation. If I don't say it now, it might seem odd when I finally do.

I must have taken too long because he laughs hesitantly. "Yeah, I know. Grim stuff to talk about so soon."

Shit. My brain scrambles to respond, and I blurt out, "No, it's fine. I didn't plan on telling you my husband died."

He's quiet for a moment before saying, "Oh damn, aren't we a pair?"

The tone of his voice has a touch of humor, and it defuses my discomfort. I laugh wryly and agree with him. We're both lost in our thoughts for several moments, but now that we've told each other about our spouses, it's like the floodgates have opened.

I tell him how I met Josh, how he died, and go into a brief explanation of how I've been doing since the accident. Noah talks about his wife, Josie, and how rough it was when they diagnosed her with triple-negative breast cancer. I want to giggle when he says her name was Josie, but he might not appreciate my playfulness. Josh and Josie? If there is a heaven, maybe they are up there laughing at us.

He doesn't talk about how much he loved her, or that he misses her, and I wonder if after ten years without someone you don't think about it anymore. I hope I never forget Josh, but I wouldn't mind if some of these painful memories faded a bit—especially the ones surrounding the accident itself.

We talk for so long I have to get a snack in the middle of it. At around the three-hour mark, we realize we should probably get on with our day. I have some chores to do around the condo before bedtime, and he needs to go to the store for more cat litter. We say goodbye, and he promises to text as soon as he gets his test results. I think that's the end of the conversation and I'm about to hang up, but he isn't done.

"Lexi, thanks for listening."

I chuckle self-consciously while pleasure hums through me. I give an awkward, "Yeah, you too," and we finally get off the phone.

Flopping back on the couch, I stare at the ceiling while my mind does pirouettes. What are the chances of meeting someone who also lost their spouse? My opinion of Noah on the first day was all wrong. Sure, he was late and he lost his keys, but maybe he's not the flighty carefree guy I took him for. The more I get to know him, the more he seems like dating material. It's a dangerous thought, and I probably shouldn't even go there. The agreement we have is a pretty sweet deal for me.

I drag myself off of the couch and start dinner. The conversation about our spouses drained the sexual tension. Now that I'm off the phone with him, I think back on how close to my orgasm I was when he told me to stop. I still need to figure out how he's turning the tables on me. In the moment, I don't notice until it's too late. One of these times, I'm going to get the upper hand and keep it.

Later that night, right before I drift off to sleep, I realize I never got him to tell me what he does for work. Dangit!

CHAPTER

Six

The next morning, I wake up already wet. A text from Noah with a screenshot of his negative test results gives me a zing. He includes a cute "How does tonight sound?" note with it. Hell, yes! Lust shoots through me, and my hands shake as I reply.

LEXI

I get off work at 7. Be here at 8:30 sharp.

I tap my finger to my lip, wondering what I should wear tonight. I want his cock in me as soon as possible and contemplate opening the door in my robe. My phone beeps with an incoming message.

NOAH

8:30 sounds good. It's a date.

The word "date" gives me a buzz. Shit, I need to get a grip. He's using the word casually. It doesn't mean what my brain thinks. I remind myself this is a temporary arrangement, but he's making it difficult not to get attached. If he would be a little more unlikeable, dammit! I giggle at the thought. I suppose it's better if the biological father of my future child isn't a jerk. DNA testing kits are pretty easy to get these days. By the time my kid is an adult, they might find Noah, especially since it sounds like they have a half-sibling already. I pause on that thought. I assume only one half-sibling. Who knows how far and wide Noah has spread his seed?

Wishing I could snuggle back in bed, I stretch and force myself to get up. I need breakfast before work. While my oatmeal is warming, I make my lunch to take with me and think about the amazing sex last weekend. A throb between my legs makes me wish I had time to rub myself, but I can't. Since he told me we're waiting until we get together for our next orgasms, it's not like I can finish myself off anyway.

I spent too much time daydreaming this morning and rush to finish my oatmeal. When I'm done eating, I bounce from foot to foot as I clean the kitchen, too energized to stay still. Noah has my head whirling, and he's not even here touching me.

After I shower, I grab my lunch and head to work. This day better go fast. It needs to be tonight already.

~

Work is slow, which makes the hours drag. I spend most of the time fantasizing about tonight. By the time my shift is over, I'm desperate for Noah's cock. At this rate, I'll orgasm with one touch.

When I get home, I take another quick shower and slip on my robe. I have three robes made of different fabrics, depending on my mood. The silk robe is for my romantic nights, while my terrycloth is for everyday. The satin one is for seduction. I'm in the satin one tonight, and I don't plan on wearing it for long.

I'm ready fifteen minutes early and sit on my couch, full of nervous energy, and check the time on my phone obsessively. He texted me once during work and told me he's looking forward to tonight. I told him I was as well. I felt unsettled today because I kept wanting to message him. How often can I text him without coming across as clingy or making him so uncomfortable he ends up saying he needs less contact between our sex dates? The agreement and subsequent conversations have me tied up in knots. I don't know where things are going with him or if they are even going anywhere. I sigh loudly and try to relax while I wait.

As the minutes tick by, my pussy gets even more wet. Since it's later at night, I assume he is already home from work, but it's possible he's coming straight here from a shift—if he even worked today. I really need to ask him what he does.

He's five minutes late when the doorbell finally rings, and my stomach does somersaults. I jump up and rush to the door, knowing I want to open it, shove him to the floor, and ride him. I look through the security peephole to verify it's him, noticing he's in jeans and a t-shirt. This means he probably wasn't at work. I loosen the belt on my robe so it gapes open. Pulling on the fabric, I adjust it so there's a line of skin visible from my neck all the way down. I want him to know I'm naked under the robe.

I open the door and smile brightly at him. The grin on his face turns feral as his eyes skim down the front of me. I think I'm about to get fucked hard. Flushing from his intense gaze, my mind blanks for a second and I say the first thing that pops into my head. "Hi, Noah. You're late."

"I am. Can I still come in?"

I nod and stand aside, holding the door open and letting him pass. The last couple of days have been like foreplay, and there is no way in hell I would send him away at this point. I lock the door and turn around right as he steps close and pulls me into his arms. I hum in pleasure from the feel of the fabric of his shirt and jeans along my exposed skin, but I desperately want him naked so I can rub my body against his.

I slide my hands under his shirt, and he uses one of his hands to tip my face up. When he claims my mouth in a kiss, desire swirls in my stomach. I moan and press against him as I caress his sides. Running my fingers through the soft hair on his chest, I imagine the friction against my bare nipples and shiver.

He breaks off the kiss and pulls the sash of my robe loose. When he nudges the fabric off my shoulders, I let it pool on the floor. He takes a step back and eyes the length of my body. I want to squirm under his gaze but hold myself still. On most days, I'm proud of the way I look, but having someone examine me this closely brings out my insecurities.

There is only appreciation in his eyes, and a warmth radiates from my core. When he reaches out and caresses his thumb across my lips, I'm breathless and vibrating with need. Why hasn't he dragged me to bed yet?

Since I can't handle any more foreplay tonight, I find my voice and purr at him. "Please don't tease me tonight. I need your cock inside me."

He raises an eyebrow and moves the hand from my face down to my nipple. He pulls at it just enough to cause a confusing mixture of pain and pleasure, and I gasp as my pussy pulses.

His voice is gravelly when he replies. "Okay, my breeding fucktoy. But first we need safewords."

An inferno of need engulfs me. *Oh, fuck yes.*

My brain blips out again, and I can't think of a safeword. I've never needed one before, so I never thought about it. Noah looks at me expectantly while I frantically search around the room to get inspiration.

He's clearly impatient when I don't have one handy. "Well, fucktoy, what will it be?"

I glance over at the fireplace and zero in on a picture that my husband, Josh, took of me at a goat farm. He used to laugh at me because I love tiny goats. If they're wearing tiny sweaters, even better.

I blurt out, "Goat," and giving Noah credit: he doesn't blink an eye.

"Okay, goat it is." He brushes a finger along my cheek, jolting me back to the present. The touch feels like electricity on my skin and pulls my attention back to him.

His eyes mesmerize, and I can't look away. God, he's got such gorgeous lashes. My entire body tingles from being near him, and I can feel wetness dripping down my inner thigh.

"Lexi?"

"Hmmm?" My voice is dreamy, and I'm in a hazy, lust-filled, happy place. I want him to bend me over the couch and fuck me right here.

"I'm giving you a ten-second head start to the bedroom. If I catch you before you're on the bed, we're going to see if you enjoy being spanked."

It takes at least one second for my mind to comprehend what he said. My eyes widen. Wait...what? I don't want to be spanked.

He tips his head towards the hallway. "You better get moving."

A surge of adrenaline hits me. I stop thinking and take off towards the bedroom, but my hesitation wasted too many seconds. He easily catches me, scoops me up as if I weigh nothing, and tosses me over his shoulder while I squeal. I'm breathless and my heart hammers in my chest, but the thrill of being caught might be worth a spanking.

He smacks my bare ass as he carries me the last few steps into the bedroom, and I yelp from the sting. Oooh, or maybe not. I'm uncertain how much I liked the one spank. How many did he say I was getting?

When he dumps me on the bed, I get a sense of déjà vu. He'd carried me into the bedroom that time, too. Maybe this is just his thing? I can be down with this hunter-prey vibe he's got going on, as long as the spanking doesn't hurt too badly.

I spread out on my side with my head on my hand and watch him take his clothes off. He's methodical and slow about it, which is not what I expected. He seems the type who would drag me in here, rip his clothes off, and ravish me. There's nothing wrong with a little striptease, and I enjoy the show.

When he pulls off his shirt, the muscles in his chest and arms ripple, and I swallow hard. My pussy buzzes when I think about running my hands up his powerful arms. If we were fucking in a chair, I'd straddle and face him so I could hold on to his yummy shoulders.

After he removes each item, he folds it and places it on the dressing chair next to my vanity. His jeans hit the floor, and when he bends over to pick them up and then twists slightly to put them on the chair, I get a very sexy view of one ass cheek. He's seen my body the two times we've been together, it's nice to check him out for a change.

His cock is erect and I imagine him walking over to me and having me sit on the edge of the bed and suck on him. The flutter from my stomach almost has me asking for it, but he breaks my train of thought.

"Get up on all fours and face your ass towards me."

Oooh, guess it's time for this spanking. I'm more turned on by this than I expected. A thrill runs through me as I scramble up on my hands and knees in the middle of the bed.

I wiggle my ass and look over my shoulder at him. "Like this?"

He's staring at my slit and seems distracted, so I shimmy my hips again. His cock twitches like it's waving hello to my pussy, and I giggle. The sound makes him focus.

His voice is deep and husky and sends a shiver down my spine. "Move back until your knees are on the edge."

I scoot backwards as he gets closer to the bed, turning my face towards the headboard. I brace myself for pain, but he surprises me by trailing his cock along my ass and then pressing the tip against the opening of my wet folds. Pushing my hips back to him, I force him inside me and groan from the pleasure.

He laughs and pulls out. "Oh, no you don't. I decide when I'm going to use my fucktoy."

He swats my ass, and I gasp. It didn't hurt; it made me want his cock inside me even more. Squirming, I wish there was some way I could entice him to skip the spanking and just fuck me. I have a crazy idea and reject it, then reconsider. Why not? What's he gonna do, spank me? Hell, I might as well try it.

Glancing over my shoulder again, I purr at him. "I think you should just forget everything and use me."

He rewards my efforts with a hard crack on my ass that makes me yelp. "Hey!"

"I already told you, I decide when to use you," he bites off as he delivers another smack to the other cheek.

Ooh, fine! I want to get bratty with him, but he spanks me, alternating sides with each swing. My brain drains of all thought as I clutch the comforter in my fists to steady myself. Each whack makes me whimper because it borders on painful pleasure. I can tell my pussy is getting wetter.

I lose track of how many times he smacks me after five, and I zone out while my mind drifts into a dream-like state where everything feels good. I'm so out of it, I don't notice when he stops until his cock presses against my opening again and pleasure washes over me.

I moan loudly in anticipation of the first full thrust, but he pauses and doesn't move any further.

"Lexi...fucktoy...you did so well with begging last time. You're going to have to beg for it again."

Ugh. What's with him and begging? I don't remember what I said last time, so I can't copy it.

I moan, "I don't—"

He cuts me off with a sharp lunge straight to my core.

"Oooh, fuck!" I cry out as he hammers against me.

He growls, "Changed my mind. I'm not waiting," as the room spins from the rush of pleasure.

All I can do is grip the comforter and brace myself as best I can as he whacks against me repeatedly. Every time he bottoms out, I gasp or moan from the intense bliss. He's fucking me hard and fast, and I can't think of anything beyond this moment and the inferno he's creating with every thrust.

"Oh, Lexi?"

"Hmmm?" I'm lost in the moment and can barely respond.

"Don't even think about coming until I say you can."

Shit! A bolt of electricity hits me with his words. It's almost as if time stands still while waves of ecstasy threaten to overtake me. I hear my cries and his moans, along with the slapping sounds of our bodies colliding, but it's all from a distance. All my senses come alive, and the smell of sex mixes with the fresh cotton scent of my clean bedding. I feel every inch of his cock while I quiver around him. My body tightens, and I groan louder when he forcefully thrusts inside of me.

When he spanks my tender ass, I inhale sharply from the pain, and I'm brought back to my body as it quickly turns to pleasure. My heart rate speeds up as I get closer to my orgasm with every plunge. I chant out, "Fuck me, Noah," and he rewards me by fucking me even harder.

When he twists a chunk of my hair in his hand and pulls my head back while continuing to hammer against me, all I can do is whimper.

His voice is harsh when he growls. "Fucktoy, do you want to come?"

The spikes of pleasure are too much and I know I'm going to come at any moment, but I pant out, "Yes, please, can I come?"

"I have one question first."

"What? Please, can I come?"

He waits for two more strokes before continuing, and I'm about to lose my mind. My body quivers with anticipation. If he said the word, I'd shatter.

"Are you," he huffs while ramming into me, "my fucktoy...that I can use...however I want?"

My head buzzes with his question. A deep realization hits me: he really could do whatever he wanted to me right now, and I would love it and beg for more.

I open my mouth to say yes, but when I take too long to reply, he yanks my hair back harder and smacks my ass again.

I yelp as he threatens, "Answer me."

I breathe out, "Yes," and it tips me over the edge.

My vision blurs, and the bliss overtakes me. My orgasm rips through me, running from my fingers all the way to my toes. I moan with delight and buck and shudder with my release. Noah doesn't stop his thrusting, and the waves continue to wash over me in a never-ending joyride.

He gives one last whack against my pussy and roars when he comes. He jerks and convulses as he unloads ropes of his hot cum deep inside me. This was the moment I've been waiting for, and knowing he's unloading everything he's got almost pushes me over the edge again. I moan in tandem with him, imagining his cum coating my inner walls.

He slows his thrusting and fucks me gently for a moment while my pussy milks every drop from him. If we were both on the bed, I'd want to spoon while he softens inside me, but I'm too hazy to ask and we're not in the right position.

When he pulls out, I collapse forward onto the bed and can't move. I don't even care that my face is squished into the comforter. I'm floating in that warm, happy place and want to live here forever.

I'm vaguely aware of him pulling me up towards the pillow, and when my head touches it, I slide my arms underneath it and settle in. I'll give myself another few minutes to enjoy how thoroughly fucked I am before moving. I don't pay attention to Noah until I feel a cool liquid on my inflamed ass.

"Wha...?" I try to look over my shoulder to see what's going on.

"I'm going to rub some lotion on you. I'll be gentle."

"Oh, okay." I bury my head in the pillow while he gently massages the lotion into both ass cheeks. It feels wonderful, and I give a faint groan. When he stops, I hear him leave the room for a few minutes. Where is he going?

He returns and sits down on the side of the bed next to me, causing the bed to dip, and I have to adjust my position so I don't slide into him.

"Lexi, I need you to sit up and take a big drink for me. Then you can lie back down."

I glance at his hands, and he's holding a glass of water and a package of crackers he must have found in my cupboard. I lick my lips and realize I'm thirsty. Ugh, this means I have to sit up.

I pull myself upright and reach for the glass. It isn't until I take it from him that I notice my hands are shaking. He helps steady the glass while I gulp a big mouthful. When I'm done, he takes it and puts a cracker in its place. I can't help but giggle at how ridiculous this is. He's taking care of me like I'm a child. At the same time, I'm flooded with a warmth that he cares about how I'm doing.

"Good girl, now eat your cracker. I want to see you eat three of them."

I don't argue and murmur, "Okay," and snuggle back down into bed. I don't need to sit up to nibble on crackers.

He takes a swig of the water he brought for me, and the intimacy of him sharing my glass makes me laugh again. He just thoroughly fucked me and somehow his drinking from the same glass strikes me as intimate?

Remembering how he left last time once the fucking was over, I expect him to say he needs to leave. I'm surprised when he climbs onto the bed with me and cuddles up close, folding his arms around me so my face is against his chest. We're both sweaty and he's almost too warm, but I don't care. I snuggle against him and close my eyes, enjoying the moment for however long it lasts while I try to work up the courage to ask him to stay the night.

We lay in silence for a bit, but when I feel him brushing the hair off my face, I crack my eyes open and look up at him.

He traces his fingertip along my jaw and asks in a coarse whisper, "Do you want me to sleep here tonight?"

I can't stop the leap of happiness that jumps into my throat, and I smile at him. "Yes, I'd like that."

Burrowing my head into his chest again, I try to hide my delight. He's staying, and I didn't have to ask him.

His voice is deep and smooth. "Were you okay with how rough I was?"

His question makes me whip my head back to look at him again. Is he crazy? How could he even wonder that? I search his face to make sure he isn't teasing me, but he looks sincere.

I smile. "Yes, it was great."

"Even the spanking?"

When he mentions the spanking, I realize my ass is sore, but I also get a nice zing at the same time.

"Oh, yes, even the spanking."

My slutty side would like to be spanked again, but I don't mention it. I'm pretty sure it's going to be a repeated occurrence. If not? I can needle him until I get what I want. I bet I'd only need to be a little defiant in the middle of sex, and I'd get rewarded with a smack on the ass.

Since he's staying all night, I don't feel rushed. I relax and let my mind drift. He's great in bed, and funny, so I'm curious why he's single. It's been over ten years since his wife died, so he's probably had other girlfriends.

I use a fingertip to draw circles on his chest and ask, "After Josie, what's the longest relationship you've had?"

He's quiet for a moment, and I assume he's thinking about a bunch of girlfriends and counting months.

"I've only had friends with benefits since Josie."

I was not expecting that answer, but why in the hell was he on a dating app for people looking for love?

I'm brave and ask him. "Why were you on THAT dating app? There are other ones for hookups."

His voice sounds amused. "I don't know. Why were YOU on that app?"

Oh, shit. I laugh, say, "Touché," and decide to change the subject. I snuggle closer against him and sigh. "This is nice."

He runs his fingers along my shoulder, tickling me a little. "I always thought if my parents spent more time in bed cuddling, maybe they wouldn't have fought so much."

Oh dang, he's talking about his past. I pry a little. "Your parents fought a lot?"

He snorts. "Oh yeah, it was horrible. I had a really fucked up childhood, and it affected my relationship with Josie. We were always fighting and miserable. I didn't know there was any other way."

I'm surprised at how articulate he's being about mistakes in the past. He's either thought a lot about this or he's had therapy. I think it's rude to ask someone if they had therapy, so I keep the thought to myself while he continues.

"I was planning on divorcing Josie, but after she got her cancer diagnosis, I didn't have the heart to do it. Once we realized it wouldn't end well, I was glad I'd never gotten up the nerve."

He falls quiet for a moment, and I kiss his chest. "That sounds really rough. I'm sorry."

Josh suddenly dying was super shitty, and I loved him dearly, but I've always wondered if watching someone grow sicker every day for weeks would be worse. I never figured out the answer, but having the chance to say goodbye would have helped give me closure. I don't think anyone can ever know how they would react until it happens, so maybe losing Josh suddenly was better. If there is a heaven, I hope he's not up there shaking his head and wondering what in the fuck I'm doing with Noah.

He plays with my hair and kisses my forehead before quietly saying, "I'm not good with relationships, so it's best if I stay single."

My heart gives a tiny pang at his words and I wonder if he's warning me not to fall for him. A small part of my brain whispers it might be too late as I fall asleep.

Seven

Tonight is the first time we're having sex when I'm fertile. I'm eager, hopeful, impatient. As he walks in the front door, I close it behind him. He grabs me and shoves me against the wall, face first, while I flatten my hands against the textured surface.

He grinds his cock against my ass, and a ripple of pleasure runs through me, centering on my clit. I try to use the wall as leverage to push back against him. I'm reminded of the elevator ride with him. He shoved me against the wall that night also and asked if I wanted him to breed me. God, it was so hot. I get a double dose of sexual zings, first from thinking about the day I met him, and also knowing I might get pregnant this time.

His hot breath is in my ear, and he growls. "Remember, your safeword is goat."

Oooh, shit. He thinks I might need my safeword? I love it when he reminds me of my safeword because it makes me imagine how hard he's going to fuck me.

Noah flips me around so I'm facing him. I tried to dress sexy casual and wore my best ass-hugging jeans and my favorite red blouse. What he hasn't discovered yet is I'm braless underneath it. I'm wearing exactly three items of clothing: the shirt, my jeans, and my sluttiest pair of thong underwear—so pointless it might as well be dental floss.

He pulls the blouse free of my jeans, and as he captures my mouth for a brutal kiss, my bare toes curl on the cold flooring in my entryway. Mmmm, I wasn't expecting to be ravished right when he walked in, but this is hot and I'm not complaining. Since I knew this night was coming, I've been getting turned on every day thinking about him fucking me and possibly getting me pregnant. Now that he's here, I'm soaking wet and ready for him.

He breaks off the kiss and sucks on my neck as he undoes my jeans. He gets them open enough to slip a hand inside and brushes the wisp of panties out of the way as he plunges a finger between my slick folds.

"Ohhh." I arch against his hand.

Noah chuckles harshly. "It looks like my little breeding fucktoy is ready to be used."

Shit, I love it when he degrades me. He does it in the perfect way that makes it sound like a filthy endearment. It wasn't a question, but I pant out a "Yes" while he fingers my pussy and sucks on my neck. I know I'm going to have marks there tomorrow, almost as if he's claiming me.

He nibbles his way up to plunder my mouth, and I'm dizzy and needy as our tongues duel. When he comes up for air, he talks to me between kisses. "Lexi...?"

"Mmmm, yes?" I moan, wishing it was his cock sliding into me instead of his finger. I'm getting the sense tonight is going to be fast and hard, and I'm ready for us both to be naked and in my bed.

He doesn't reply for a moment, alternating between rubbing my clit and slipping a finger inside to massage my sensitive spot. My body tenses as the pleasure builds in my core. Holy fuck, he's already got me close to coming.

"Lexi." His voice is almost a growl again and I shiver from the primal tone. "Ask me to breed you."

My head spins at his words and all I can do is groan against his mouth. "Yes."

"No, ask me," he demands. "I want to hear you say it."

He breaks off the kiss. I open my mouth to speak, but he roughly plunges two fingers into my pussy instead of one. I cry out from the intense, painful pleasure as he starts finger fucking me aggressively. Fuuuck, this is so amazing.

"Say it, or I'll stop."

Squirming and moaning loudly against the pleasurable assault, I close my eyes and embrace the sluttiness of what we're doing.

"Noah," I gasp out as a gnawing need overwhelms me, "breed me please."

He stops kissing me, removes his fingers from my jeans, and gives a soft laugh. Wait, what's this? I open my eyes and focus on him while he kisses my nose. His switch from dominating to soft confuses my brain, and I don't know what to think.

He starts out sounding amused, "Yes, I'm going to breed you..." and then his voice turns deep. "Hard."

When Noah says the word 'hard,' he seizes the silky fabric of my button-down blouse in both fists and splits it open. The silk rips and some buttons fall on the floor with a clatter. I gasp and realize I've never had anyone destroy a shirt during sex before. The wild savageness thrills me, and I don't mourn the demise of my favorite shirt.

"Oooh, nice," he groans when he's presented with my generous, bare breasts. Cupping both my tits, he rolls my nipples between his thumbs and index fingers with a delicious roughness while I writhe against his hands.

He's wearing entirely too many clothes, and I pluck at his shirt, knowing I won't get it off, but maybe he'll help me.

My efforts only make him snicker. "Patience, my little fucktoy. We'll both be naked soon."

He stops playing with my breasts and kisses down my stomach, getting on his knees as he peels the jeans down my legs.

"I like this." He traces the top edge of the triangle of black fabric barely covering my pussy, and his breath tingles my skin as he helps me step out of the jeans.

I'm curious if he's going to rip my thong off like he did with my shirt, but he grasps the top edge and pulls up. It digs between my pussy lips and almost grazes my clit. I gasp and jerk my hips, hoping I can get it to rub on the perfect spot.

"Spread your legs," he commands. I quickly obey as he leans in and licks around the stretched fabric.

"Oooh, my god," I moan out and move my hands to his head, running my fingers through his hair as he sucks on my clit.

I was already close to my orgasm, and this spirals me even higher. Closing my eyes again, I buck my hips against his face. The tendrils of delight gather with every passing second.

When he stops licking me and sits back on his knees, I take a moment to realize he's stopped.

Ugh, fuck. I open my eyes and look down at him. His feral gaze locks onto mine.

"Lexi, we're going to go into the bedroom, and I'm going to use you like the fucktoy you are."

My pussy throbs as he speaks, and I almost moan as he continues.

"You're going to enjoy every thrust...every pulse...when I come, it's going to be so hard you're going to feel my cum filling you up and overflowing, dripping out of your pussy."

His filthy words ping something in my brain, and my mouth falls open and I peep out a tiny, "Oh," as my mind shuts off. I am his fucktoy, and I'm desperate for his cum.

He stands up and holds his hand out to me. "You ready to be bred?"

My senses come alive with a whoosh. My body tingles, and I'm sensitive to the movement of air. I can hear the furnace kick on and Noah's breathing. I've been ready for this moment for weeks now.

Thinking about how exhilarating it was to be chased to the bedroom, I decide I want that excitement again. Instead of taking his hand, I slap it and pretend to be defiant. "We'll see. If you can catch me, you can breed me."

I don't wait for him to respond before sprinting towards the bedroom. I make it part of the way down the hallway before he catches up with me. With a roar, he picks me up and throws me over his shoulder like I'm a sack of potatoes. My pulse races, and I'm grinning widely.

"Caught you," he growls and smacks my ass. I laugh as he carries me into the bedroom.

There are some definite advantages to having a muscular guy as my breeding partner. His ability to carry me around is hot. I pretend to be the helpless woman he's taking advantage of, which hits a nice kink of mine. Expecting to be tossed on the bed, I'm surprised when he lowers my feet to the floor and keeps me stable until I can stand on my own.

I continue to poke at the bear. "So, big boy, you caught me. Now what?"

He grips my shoulders, pivots me until I'm facing the bed, and shoves my head down so I'm leaning with my ass in the air. I rest on my forearms and wiggle my hips at him. Every nerve ending is on fire and I'm so wet he could slide right in with no more foreplay.

His voice is calm, which contrasts with how primal he's sounded. "Now, you're going to behave and do everything I say. Because if you don't, I'm going to pull out and come anywhere I feel like, except your pussy."

What's this? He's got to come inside me. That was the agreement.

"Hey," I whine, "you're supposed to breed me and get me pregnant —not come anywhere else!"

Noah laughs. "Then you better do exactly what I tell you to do."

He yanks down my panties and nudges my legs apart with his knee while the room spins. I put my hands on the comforter, resting my forehead on them while sucking in some air. I want to give him the best angle to get his seed deep inside me.

I wait for him to plow into me and start hammering against my pussy. Instead, he smacks my pussy lips, and I buck my ass up involuntarily from the sharp pleasure.

My "Oomph" is muffled, and I'm about to beg. My pussy spasms from need, and I'm desperate for his cock and cum.

I hear him removing his clothes. The rustle of the fabric is erotic as I imagine it brushing across his skin before he drops it to the floor. I've got it bad for Noah. No guy has ever turned me on this much.

He presses against my ass and rubs his erection lengthwise along my folds and bumps the head of his cock against my clit. "Mmmm," I moan. God, he's so close. If I could bend over fully and touch my ankles, maybe he'd slip inside me.

I'm surprised when Noah reaches forward and runs his hands underneath me and plays with my tits. He cups their fullness and plays with the stiff peaks, giving them a tug that borders on painful but isn't quite.

"Lexi, in a few months, you're going to be pregnant and your nipples are going to be so full and sensitive. Have you imagined what that's going to feel like?"

Oooh, what's this? I think about what he described and imagine him sucking on my nipples, and my pussy clenches. A tiny zip of pleasure runs straight from my breasts to my clit.

He pulls on my nipples some more, and his voice is harsh when he asks again. "Have you thought about it?"

Grinding back against him, I pant out, "Fuck...yes!"

I shift my ass, hoping he'll slide his cock inside me, but he doesn't. He runs his hands down my sides, tickling me, and I almost giggle. He stops and kneads my belly.

"Think of how full your belly is going to be when I'm done with you. I'm going to fill you up and make you feel so good."

What the hell is happening here? Everything he's saying would sound stupid and hilarious in any other context, but right here, right now? It's working me into a frenzy. I can barely think. I just want his cum inside me.

Noah presses firmly on my belly and nudges his cock against my wet entrance. Tendrils of pleasure ripple through me as he continues. "I've been saving my cum for days now, waiting for tonight when I can pump you so full it's going to drip out of you and run down your legs."

I get a very clear visual of what he's saying, and as soon as I imagine all that cum, I reach my breaking point. I whimper, "God, Noah. Please fuck me...please?" and try to press back against the head of his cock.

"Hmmm, Lexi. I don't know if you want it bad enough yet."

"What?" Fuuuuck. I rotate my hips, forcing the head into my pussy slightly, but with his hand on my stomach and him pressing against my ass, I can't move enough to get any relief. Each tiny movement makes my pussy ripple with pleasure. It won't take me long to orgasm once he finally thrusts inside me.

"Please Noah? I'll do anything...anything you want. Just fuck me, please?"

He presses his cock in part of the way as electricity builds in my core. "Anything?"

"Ooooh, god. Please, fuck me. Anything!"

My nipples pucker and my thighs quiver, while my cave walls spasm around his half-buried cock.

He sounds entirely too controlled when he speaks to me, and my head swims from how needy I am in comparison. "That's because you're a cock-hungry slut. Aren't you?"

He moves his hands to my hips, and as he presses in further, I moan, "Yes."

"Say it, Lexi." His voice is harsh, and his tone thrills me.

I bounce my hips, realizing I can get a little movement that way, and it ignites an inferno of need in me. "I'm a cock-hungry slut. Now please fuck me!"

Noah laughs. "Not yet, my breeding fucktoy. You're desperate for this, aren't you?"

I mewl out a tiny, "Yes," and he continues on. "You really need my cum inside you right now, don't you?"

Oh, fuck. I writhe underneath him, trying to spear his cock in further, and hear myself faintly reply, "Yes."

"Every instinct is telling you that my cum is what you need."

The pressure in my core is close to erupting. I'm not sure how much longer I can wait. I'm desperate for his cum and an orgasm. "Fuck... yes...please."

He slides in, and I groan loudly when he bottoms out. Instead of thrusting again, he pauses. "You want to know what's going to happen?"

I peep out a small, "What?" and buck my hips, forcing him to knock against me deep inside.

Noah withdraws fully and then slams back into me. Ooooooh, fuck!

"You are going to be a beautiful pregnant mess when I'm done with you."

"Yeesss," I breathe out and clutch the comforter in my fists while he hammers into me.

My thighs quiver uncontrollably with every thrust, and my body tightens. I chant, "Yes," repeatedly. He whacks against me, hitting the magical spot, and I moan with delight.

Noah moans with me, and the sound of him slapping against my wet pussy fills the room. I'm so close to coming and fully focused on the mounting pleasure that when he smacks my ass, I yelp loudly from the pain.

"It's time for my fucktoy to come, and when you do, I'm going to breed this pretty little pussy of yours."

My mind freezes for a moment. When he rams against me, it pushes me over the edge and my orgasm rips through me. Waves of bliss wash over me, and I spiral higher and higher as he pounds against my pussy.

With a loud groan, he shudders, and the warmth of his seed coats my inner walls. I enjoy every spurt as my pussy clenches and milks him. I continue to tremble with an orgasm that feels like it's never going to end as he fucks his cum back up inside of me.

When he finally slows his thrusts, I'm still quivering with tiny aftershocks of pleasure. His cock gives a couple final twitches before he pulls out. Wetness runs down my thigh, and imagining I'm losing all his cum makes me scramble on the bed. I plop on my back and lie still, hoping tonight is the night I finally get pregnant.

Noah crawls up next to me and collapses with a groan. I turn my head to look at him. His eyes are closed, and those gorgeous eyelashes of his stand out. He's smiling, so I know he had a good time. I sigh, contentedly, and close my eyes as well and let myself drift in my bubble of happiness while I think about all the things Noah said to me. That man has a filthy mouth, but fuck if I didn't love it.

CHAPTER
Eight

We arranged for him to stay the weekend with the goal of having tons of sex. I wake the next morning with him spooning me and his erect cock against my ass. As soon as he can tell I'm awake, he kisses my shoulder.

"Good morning," he murmurs and nibbles his way across my upper back to my neck.

"Mmmm." He slips his hand over my breast and toys with my nipple.

My brain is barely awake, but my body zings alive at his touch and I can tell I'm already wet. I remember how long he teased me last night and don't want to risk it happening again, so I remove his hand from my breast and force it between my legs.

He doesn't need any further prompting, and I sigh in delight as he slips his fingers between my wet folds and caresses my clit gently. His cock pulses against my ass. I shift positions slightly and adjust my leg so he can slide into my pussy from behind. I love how thick he is and the ripples of ecstasy as he stretches me. All it takes is him sinking into me fully and I'm cock-drunk from the pleasure.

We rock together, slowly and sensually, while he rubs my swollen clit and gentle waves of pleasure wash over me. I'm a little sensitive from last night, so waking up like this is perfect.

He keeps a steady pace until the end, when he pushes me onto my stomach, covers me with his body, and thrusts hard and fast. I come with an intensity I wasn't expecting, and the release makes me giggle. I'm not sure if the laughing did it for him, but he moans as his cock spasms and his warm cum floods my pussy.

I'm still giggling in small bursts when he rolls onto his back. I snuggle against him with my head on his chest.

"Now that's the right way to wake up," I tease between my fits of laughter.

"Mm hmm," he replies as he caresses my back, lost in either thought or bliss. I can't tell which one it is yet.

His stomach growls against my ear, which sets off my funny bone again.

I'm still laughing when I sit up. "Why don't I make us some breakfast?"

"Do you mind if I shower while you do that?" He gets up with me, and even though we didn't cuddle that long, the morning still has an intimacy I've missed while single.

I slip on my robe and show him where I keep the towels, letting him know he can use any bathroom supplies he wants. When he came over last night, he didn't have a bag with him, so I wonder if he plans on returning to his house today to get his things.

I begin making cheese omelets and, as I'm cracking the eggs, I pause. Wait, what if he doesn't really plan on staying? I didn't verify with him he was going to sleep over, and his lack of overnight bag perplexes me. Maybe he forgot? I'm not sure how I feel about this, and I stew about it while I make breakfast.

When he joins me, he kisses my cheek and says, "Smells good," while he gropes my ass through the fabric of my robe.

Having Noah in my kitchen settles me and puts an extra jaunt in my step. I dish up the omelets and pour us glasses of orange juice before we sit down at the small kitchen table to eat.

"Were you planning on staying the night tonight as well?" I try to keep my voice casual, but I'm not sure I succeed.

"I need to talk to you about that."

My stomach drops, and I didn't realize how much I was looking forward to him being here all weekend until that moment.

"Oh?" I take a bite of my food to prove this conversation doesn't matter to me.

"Yeah, a guy at work is sick, so they asked if I could come in for a couple of hours today. I thought I could grab clothes for tomorrow after work and come back."

Oh yuck, he has to work. But I perk up; wait, this is my chance to find out what he does.

"Where do you work?"

I almost don't enjoy asking him because it's a reminder of how little we know about each other. I'm getting to learn what makes the inner Noah tick, but he's very closemouthed about the details of his life.

He takes a sip of orange juice before answering. "I freelance with a PI firm."

Wait, what the hell is a PI firm? Like a private investigator on TV? He must be able to tell I'm confused.

"I'm a private investigator."

I blink at him while I wonder if this should impress me. Being a private investigator sounds important, but it could be one of those jobs that anyone can make a business card for and call themselves one.

"How long have you been a PI?"

"About eighteen years. Right about the time I realized being a cop wasn't for me."

I pause with my fork halfway to my mouth. "You were a cop?"

He snorts. "No, I was in training and decided I was too much of a free spirit to be confined by the expectations of an employer."

Okay, yeah, that seems like something a younger Noah would think based on what I learned about him so far.

"So what do you do as a PI?" I've watched enough TV to know there are a lot of different things he could do. I half hope he says he hunts down cheating spouses.

"Nothing too exciting, though my specialty is proving people are cheating."

Oh, fuck yeah, I knew it! A warmth of happiness spreads through me, and I almost laugh at how stupidly excited I am that he tracks down cheaters.

"It's mostly boring work while I try to catch them in the act. Occasionally, I have to testify if the cheating spouse still fights the divorce settlement."

Huh, wonder what sort of money a PI makes. I'd never ask him, and it doesn't really matter, but if he's been doing it for eighteen years, he must make enough to live on.

"Do you like being a PI?"

He smiles. "I do. I'm good at it, so it's satisfying. I usually set my own hours, but another PI at the firm is on an important case and they begged me to help this weekend. I'll only be gone a couple of hours and then I'll come back and fuck you silly again. Does that sound okay?"

I grin at him. "It's a date."

Noah's late, no surprises there, but at least this time he texts me to let me know he's been held up at work, so I know I have time to take a quick shower to pass the time. Afterwards, I settle down wearing nothing but a cotton nightgown, hoping he still has plans to ravish me. I'm lounging on the couch with an e-reader in my hand when I hear the spare key I gave him slide into the lock and he walks into the living room a moment later.

He's carrying a small duffle bag that he drops on the floor in the entryway.

"Hey, sorry I'm late."

Since he texted me as soon as he realized he'd be late, I don't mind. It gave me some time to think about the future and hope I'm already pregnant. "It's fine. I've been reading and relaxing." I tip my e-reader up towards him as if to prove what I was doing.

Noah's wearing jeans and a t-shirt. Now that I know he's a PI, I'm guessing it's what he usually wears to work. He kicks off his shoes, and when he unbuckles his belt, my body perks up. Is he stripping all the way or only getting a little more comfortable?

As he takes the belt out of his pants, I envision him using it to bind my wrists. This is probably why certain social media circles go crazy over pictures of guys holding onto a belt. Being with someone that you can imagine having such control is incredibly seductive. I have never been with anyone as powerful in bed as Noah, and now I'm unsure I could be satisfied with anything less.

The corners of his mouth curl upwards as he takes his time undressing, crossing his arms over his chest and lifting his shirt from his body. He exposes his chest inch by inch, and I hum my appreciation as his chest muscles ripple. A warmth invades my core, and my pussy grows wet. Mmm, if he would get his sexy ass over here, I could lick those delicious abs. I prop myself up so I can fully enjoy the seductive striptease.

He unzips his jeans as he comes towards me. "Work sucked. It was boring, and I couldn't stop thinking about fucking you."

"Oh?" I didn't think he was going to walk in the door and jump me, but I like where this is going.

He shoves his jeans and boxers down and kicks them off. His cock springs free, and I can see the glint of pre-cum on the head. Licking my lips, I'm about to ask if he wants to move to the bedroom, but he grabs my legs, hooks his hands around my calves, and tugs me down on the couch. My nightgown rides up and exposes my lack of panties.

His grin turns into a sexy smirk. "Looks like someone is ready for me."

I laugh. "You said you were going to fuck me when you got back."

He murmurs, "Mmm hmm," as he climbs on top of me and nestles between my legs. He rubs his cock against my slick folds, but doesn't push in. I kept thinking about him while he was gone, but all my fantasies involved the bed. I didn't even consider the couch. Noah pressed against me is better than anything I daydreamed about.

We kiss and he coaxes my lips open so he can swirl his tongue with mine. My pussy hums, and an inferno of need ignites in my core. He grinds the length of his shaft against my pussy lips, but there isn't any chance he'll accidentally slip in. I try to buck against him, seeing if that will ease my ache, but it only turns me on more.

When he runs a hand under the nightgown and up my stomach, it tickles. I giggle and squirm, causing more friction against my pussy. God, I need him to be inside me.

His hand seeks my breast, cupping it gently before playing with my nipple and making me moan. Why didn't he just open my legs and shove his cock into me? I'm feeling slutty this weekend, and I'll do whatever I can to get his cum inside me. He doesn't need to drag this out. He could fuck me multiple times every day for his pleasure, and I'd be happy as long as I ended up with a pussy full of cum. Not that I'm disliking what he's doing, but I want him to fuck me hard and fast.

I moan, "Noah, I need you inside me. Please?"

He's never given in when I ask the first time and I'm not expecting it to work, so I gasp loudly when he shifts and plunges his cock straight to my core.

"Ooooh, fuck!" I cry out as he plows into me and tugs on my nipple at the same time. I rest my hands on his shoulders and arch against him, trying to get him as deep inside me as I can while I wrap my legs around his midsection.

He might have started out slow, but as soon as he's inside me, he escalates his thrusts until he's hammering against my pussy. The room spins as the ecstasy builds. I writhe underneath him, trying to keep him inside me as long as possible.

I alternately chant, "Fuck me," and, "Oh, my god," as I spiral closer to my orgasm. When he pulls out fully and then impales me again, a sharp twinge of pleasurable pain almost sends me over the edge. He yanks my nightgown up to expose my breasts and sucks on the one he isn't playing with. I run my fingers through his hair as my mind blanks of all thoughts except my pleasure.

When he moves a hand between us and brushes a finger against my clit, I surrender to the ecstasy. I quiver around his cock and ride the waves of rapture. As soon as he can tell I'm coming, he stops caressing my clit and focuses on speeding up his thrusts. Panting, he doesn't stop until he spasms and groans, coating my inner walls with his hot cum.

He continues to drive into me slowly, and our eyes lock onto each other. His smoldering gaze is feral, and a fluttering in my stomach tells me I enjoy this primal side of him.

I draw his head down to me and kiss him deeply until he breaks it off. Nibbling his way to my neck, he brings his finger back to my clit and rubs soft circles around it. I moan softly and he whispers into my ear.

"Mine."

I breathe out, "Yes," knowing that for this weekend, I'm his and I'll do whatever he wants.

CHAPTER

Nine

Staring down at the negative pregnancy test, a loud "Shit" bursts out of my mouth. Since I live alone, I don't have to pretend everything is fine. My breath hitches and my body feels heavy as I check the test again. Yep, still negative. I'm not sure why I'm surprised since I've done this so many times in the last seven months. The sex with Noah is spectacular. In my mind, that somehow meant I'd get pregnant, when I know it doesn't work that way.

Dropping my head, I close my eyes for a moment and hopelessness washes over me. I toss the offending white stick in the trash and hold myself together until I get to my room and curl up on the bed. Clutching a pillow around my midsection, I let the tears flow freely. Why can't anything ever go my way? Every time I think I might finally get something I want in life, something bad happens.

The last few weeks with Noah have been idyllic, and I've lived in a happy bubble imagining I was pregnant after our amazing weekend together. He was attentive and asked me how I was doing every day. The times he came over for our regular twice-weekly sex were passionate and wild. He stayed the night every time, and I had to keep telling myself he wasn't my boyfriend.

He knows I planned to take an early pregnancy test today and is probably sitting at work wondering about the results. I let myself wallow a little longer before blowing my nose and picking up my phone to text him. I give a bitter smile at my screen when the text message icon shows I already have a text from him.

NOAH

Yes or no?

It's odd to know he isn't as emotionally invested in the results as I am. I want to believe I mean more to him than just a fucktoy he uses twice per week, but it's difficult to tell since he's never said he feels otherwise. He obviously enjoys my friendship, and sometimes it seems like he wants more. I mean, yes, he made it clear from the beginning he's not interested in a relationship, but...I'm uncertain what to expect when I answer him. I don't want to make him wait any longer, so I type out my response.

LEXI

It was negative.

He better not give me some stupid platitude or, worse yet, sound excited because this means he gets to fuck me more. He's fast to reply.

NOAH

Boo. I'm sorry, that sucks. You okay?

Imagining his booing brings a tiny smile to my face. Yeah, he's adorable.

LEXI

I'm a little sad, but I'll be fine. I always am.

Since tomorrow is Friday and he selected it for his twice weekly sex appointment, I want to make sure he knows he's still welcome to come over. I will not back out on my end of the deal the last week of the month because I didn't get pregnant and I'm upset about it. I send another message.

LEXI

I still want to see you tomorrow like usual.
Nothing has changed.

The indicator message shows he's typing for a bit before his message appears.

Oh, fuck. Why does he have to be so perfect? I cry again, and the water blurs my vision, making it hard to see my screen.

He probably thinks he has to give up sex for the night because he doesn't want to seem like an asshole. His reply makes me grin through the tears.

I snort. He's so totally going to order pizza, and I already know what movie I'm picking. I sniffle and wipe my nose on the back of my hand but manage a tiny giggle as I text.

His reply makes me outright laugh. It's a selfie with an exaggerated frown and a caption.

He's a bit of a goof, and I love it.

LEXI

Have fun at work. I like garlic cheesy
bread too!

I tack on a winking emoji and set my phone down. His response comforts me. A movie and pizza night is exactly what I need. A small part of me hopes he's scrambling right now to figure out what other type of takeout he can order instead of pizza. No way is he cooking me a meal.

~

When I hear Noah's key in the door, I stand from the couch and smile at him. My smile falters slightly when I see he's carrying a grocery bag and not takeout.

"Wait, you're really cooking?"

"Yep, and it's going to be delicious." He winks at me on the way to the kitchen.

I follow him, intrigued by the turn of events. I was so positive he wasn't going to cook and prepared to razz him all night about the takeout. It'll be a pleasant surprise to see a different side of him.

"Hey, do you have an apron I can wear?"

He pulls ground beef, bacon, and an onion out of the bag while I grab an apron from the walk-in pantry. I purposely give him a frilly pink one that looks like what a housewife in 1950 would wear.

He glances at it and grins while he drapes the strap over his head. He ties the strings in the back and gives me a little twirl.

"How do I look?"

Damn, he's sexy. I giggle at him. "You look like a pretty princess."

He barks out a laugh. "Just the look I was going for."

He pulls out a spatula I can tell isn't new, and I tease him. "I have spatulas here, you know."

He grabs a cutting board and knife, and starts chopping the onion into thin slices. I can tell by his precision with the knife that he knows what he's doing. "You don't have *this* spatula. This is my favorite for flipping burgers."

I don't argue with him. He can keep his illusion about his special spatula. I cook, but it's usually one-pot recipes or something I can throw in the crockpot.

I'm not sure what to do with myself while he's doing all the work. "Can I help with anything?"

He pauses his chopping to look at me. "Yes, you can sit your butt in that chair and keep me entertained while I make you a gourmet meal."

He gestures towards one of the bar stools across from him, and I take a seat. There's something about a man being domestic that makes my heart melt. Resting my elbows on the counter, I prop my chin with my hands and settle in to watch.

I'm fascinated as Noah flips hamburger patties in a skillet on the stove. He's clearly made these often, but I can't help joking with him because we both know his burgers aren't known anywhere. "What makes these world-famous?"

He's got a second skillet going to soften onions, and he stirs them before answering. "Well, technically, these aren't. You're going to have to come over to my house for that."

Whoa, what's this? I've never been to his house. "What's so different at your place that would make them famous?"

He tosses a smile at me over his shoulder. "My grill."

"Don't you think that if you could make such fabulous burgers, the grill wouldn't matter? I think you're looking for excuses in case this meal sucks."

I appreciate that he's being cute and distracting me, but his boasting is making me expect a horrible dinner.

"Oh, Lexi, that's where you're wrong. To make smash burgers, you need a grill with high enough heat that it can sear the outside of the meat in a few minutes. That's how you get the wonderful crust. These will be normal burgers—still tasty, but not the same."

Uh, what the hell is a smash burger? He stirs the onions again and turns around to lean against the counter and look at me. "Now do you see why these won't be as good?"

I bite back a grin, and my eyes sparkle. "Is now a good time to tell you I've never had a smash burger?" We'll leave out the part where I don't even know what one is. His explanation gave me a vague idea.

He mockingly gasps. "Do you want to stay the night at my place next Friday? I'll make you the real thing for dinner."

Oooh, he *is* inviting me over. I try to sound nonchalant. "Now you have to. You've bragged so much about these burgers. I have to taste them."

"Good, then it's happening." He comes over and kisses my nose before checking on the meat.

Does him inviting me over mean anything? Fuck, Lexi, you need to get a grip and stop assuming shit means more than it does. He probably just trusts me now, when he didn't know me well before. I could have been a psycho for all he knew.

I keep a smile plastered on my face while he finishes so that if he turns around, he can't tell I'm having a major internal crisis about his offer. I'm sure it's because I've had an emotional two days. Soon, I'll be more myself again.

Once the burgers are done, we fix up our buns and head out to the living room with our plates and drinks. I have TV trays so we can sit on the couch and watch the movie while we eat. We've both seen it before, but it's still nice watching it with him since it's our first time together. I snicker at myself. *The first time.* As if this is going to happen multiple times.

The burger is tasty. As we eat, I catch him glancing at me as if he's gauging my reaction. He's obviously curious whether I like it, but he's not asking. After he looks at me a third time, I decide to put him out of his misery.

"These burgers aren't half bad."

He chuckles. "Glad you approve."

He keeps grinning as he eats, as if he's happy I like it, and focuses on the movie. When we're done eating, we stretch out lengthwise on the couch and spoon, him behind me, and finish the movie that way. He keeps his arm draped over my waist, so it feels like he's hugging me and a few times he kisses my ear.

It's been so long since I've watched a movie with someone like this. I haven't dated anyone since my husband died. There was no point in taking the guys I hooked up with out on movie dates since you can't legally fuck in a movie theater. Snuggling on the couch with Noah feels right when it probably shouldn't, and I'm a bundle of mixed emotions when the movie ends.

When I turn the TV off, he yawns. "I vote we move to the bed."

Sleepy Noah is adorable. The softness on his face, with his gorgeous eyes, gives him an innocent appearance, and I can picture him as a little boy. He's so dominating in the bedroom, and the contrast with how he acts when we're not having sex is hard to wrap my head around. I always thought that guys who liked control wanted it all the time, but sleepy Noah isn't looking to dominate anyone.

My point is further proven when we get into bed and he cuddles against me with his head under my arm and resting on the side of my boob. I run my fingers through his hair, and his even breathing tells me he's asleep or close to it. Yeah, he's a cuddler. I'm not sure I really understood that until tonight. I always assumed he was giving me aftercare from the rough sex. I stroke his head some more, and I smile when he snores softly while a warmth spreads through me.

I pause my hand suddenly.

Oh, fuck.

I love him.

CHAPTER
Ten

I go to his place for smash burgers the next weekend, like he promised, and I admit they're tasty. He keeps trying to make me repeat the words, "You were right." When I refuse, he carries me to the bedroom and edges me until I finally scream it out. After he lets me come, I orgasm so hard I swear I see stars. He sure loves to control my orgasms, but I suspect he's all talk. I don't believe he'd ever not let me come. He seems to enjoy my reaction to thinking he's going to stop me.

He lives in a modest three-bedroom home with a small fenced-in yard. He surprised me with how clean and well-kept his house was. Since he's mentally scattered sometimes and is more of a free spirit, I imagined his house would be an eclectic mess. Instead, it's well organized and spotless. I don't even find anything when I peer into his closet and the bathroom cupboards. Yeah, I couldn't help it. I expected to find jumbled piles after he tossed everything in there to hide it, but nope, Noah is a tidy person.

The next few weeks are amazing. Trying to get pregnant with him is an enjoyable adventure, and we continue to have fabulously rough sex. My period comes like clockwork, but even that doesn't upset me as much as it would have before the romantic movie night.

We're coming up to my next fertile window any day now, and he's asked me to meet him for coffee at the café we went to on our first date. He didn't call it that; he said, "the café we both like," but my brain keeps thinking of it as our first date.

I'm not sure why he invited me here. I peek at my phone. He's already five minutes late. I sigh and take a sip of my chai tea. This might be something I need to accept about him. So far, he's never been over fifteen minutes late, but hopefully this isn't him still trying to make a good impression. Sometimes you date someone and their bad habit is worse the longer you stay with them...if we were dating. Fuck, I need to stop thinking this way.

When Noah breezes in a minute later, he waves at me and gives me a quick kiss before standing in line to order. I'm reminded it wasn't long ago when we were sitting here and I was admiring his sexy body while he leaned against the counter. I catch a woman at a table close by eyeing him and murmuring to another woman sitting with her. Both women check him out before giggling and whispering.

A zing of pleasure runs through me, knowing other women want my man. I try to hide my smile behind the cup as Noah slides into the chair across from me.

He can tell I'm amused at something and raises his eyebrows. "What's got you all tickled?"

I don't want to tell him I saw the other women checking him out because he might look at them, and what if he finds one of them attractive? My goal isn't to set him up with anyone else.

I shrug and go for casual. "Nothing. I'm just in a good mood today."

He looks as if he's about to say something, so I try to distract him. "Hey, what are we doing here, anyway? Afraid to be alone with me because you can't keep your hands to yourself?"

It's pretty much true. Other than the night we watched the movie, every time we're together we end up fucking, even if we don't mean to. Our agreed-upon two times per week has turned into three times. We usually plan to eat dinner or catch a movie together and then end up in some kinky position around my condo. I won't complain about having too much great sex. If I told him I couldn't see him on a particular night, I know he'd be fine with it.

He laughs at my comment. "No, I wanted to find out when would be a good time for me to take a trip. I need to be gone for a week."

"Oh." My heart drops, and I'm not sure why, but I'm immediately disappointed. Why couldn't he have texted me the question? You're an idiot, Lexi. You're acting like this is a date, and he just wants to talk about the logistics of our agreement.

Sipping my tea, I gather my thoughts before answering him. "After my next fertile days would be fine. I'll either be pregnant or we'll have a few weeks before I need you again."

I almost wince when I hear myself. I hope I didn't make it sound like I only wanted his cum. It may have started that way, but my recent revelation that I'm in love with him changes everything. Besides, we're friends now, so I wouldn't want to make him feel that way even if I wasn't in love with him. He's no Craig.

Fucking Craig. I giggle into my cup.

Noah's eyebrows furrow, and he studies me for a moment. Oh fuck, does he think I'm laughing because he's leaving and I'm talking about not needing his cum? Shit, what was the last thing I said before I giggled?

He's hesitant when he explains. "I don't think I'll be gone for more than a week. Does this sound good to you?"

I nod and pretend I'm totally fine. It seems like he's specifically not telling me where he's going or why, and I refuse to ask. He could have said what he was doing, so he obviously doesn't want to. We drink in silence for a few minutes. I notice one of the two women who were checking him out is still glancing over. A possessiveness creeps over me, and I want to link my fingers with his on top of the table to claim ownership, but I don't have that right. His lack of communication has made it pretty clear he doesn't feel like I should know where he's going or why.

We make small talk until I need to leave. I'm doing another mid shift at work. I stand up to kiss him goodbye, but he doesn't get up with me.

"Oh, you're staying?" I try to keep the surprise out of my voice.

He smiles, and I notice his gorgeous eyes again. "I'm going to reply to a few work emails and get another coffee. Text me after work, so I know you got home safely."

His request surprises me and I give an automatic response. "Sure, I'll let you know."

I walk out of the café mechanically while my thoughts whirl. I'm so confused. Is he trying to be a nice guy, or does he actually care for me? I don't want to ruin what we have by asking since he was firm about not wanting a relationship. I exhale loudly and head towards home to get ready for work.

❧

The next morning, I'm half-awake when I stumble into the bathroom. I always use the ovulation tests in the morning, and I'm usually groggy. When the ovulation kit gives me a positive result, a jolt of adrenaline shocks me awake. My stomach flutters, and I want to dance around the bathroom. Last month, I loved the rough fucking Noah gave me, so not only am I getting fabulous sex tonight, but I might also get pregnant. It's double the pleasure.

Whenever someone comes inside me and I could get pregnant, it's a naughty thrill, and it's been that way even when I didn't want a baby. I tried to explain it to a friend once, but she has actively tried not to get pregnant her entire life. Hearing that someone finds the risk exciting isn't something she can relate to. I got my kicks in college by fantasizing that my birth control failed. Who needs the actual baby when you can imagine getting pregnant and still get the rush?

Since I had been career driven when I was younger, I knew getting pregnant wasn't an option I wanted, but I still secretly hoped it would happen. If the universe made that sperm get around my birth control, then it was meant to be. I did nothing to make it fail and even had Josh wear condoms the few times it would have been unsafe. I was a little too practical to mess up my career plans and thought I had plenty of time.

Today differs from all the other times and all the other men. I didn't know I was in love with Noah last month, so toss in the possibility of getting pregnant by the man you love? Oh yeah, tonight is going to be exciting. And if the result is my arms around a baby with Noah's eyelashes, even better.

I haven't even left the bathroom yet; I'm that distracted by my thoughts. Is he going to make me beg again? My pussy buzzes and my nipples harden as I text him.

LEXI

It's a green light. Hope you're up for fucking me tonight. Get it...UP for? Yes, I know I'm hilarious.

I chuckle at how silly I am while I wait for his reply.

NOAH

I'm UP for the challenge. I'll see you after work.

Noah's reply warms my heart. I send him a kissing face emoji and set my phone down on the bathroom counter. Fuck yeah. When the desire to dance hits again, I do a little jig around the room. I'm flushed and beaming when I glance in the mirror. Ugh, why do I have to work today? Noah does too, so it's not like he'd be over here fucking me anyway, but I'm going to be distracted. As a pharmacist, that's not good.

I'll pull my shit together before work, but for now, I want to revel in the excitement. Even after all those months when I didn't get pregnant and the heartbreak from knowing I had to try again, the joy of it possibly happening is worth the pain. I'm sure it will get old at some point, but I'm not there yet and hopefully never will be.

And this might be filthy to admit, but I love it when he calls me a breeding fucktoy—and when he does it while I can get pregnant, it's fabulous. Now I understand why some women want to be pregnant all the time. If I get what I want and Noah and I stay together after this, every time he calls me a breeding fucktoy, I'm going to want to be one.

Wait, did I just think, 'if Noah and I stay together after this'? My eyes widen, and I stare at myself in the mirror, stunned. Is that what I want? I never thought too closely about what falling in love with Noah meant, and it was only a vague idea, but I mean, obviously that's what it means, right?

I was hoping he'd want to be with me once I got pregnant, but staying with him and having his baby is pretty serious. As I've gotten to know him better, I recognize he isn't going to walk away from a child after he's bonded with them, even if things don't work out with us. This goes way beyond our no-strings-attached agreement, and I'd be giving up the idea of being the only one who had any say in the child's life.

My breath is shallow, and my heart races while my head spins. I hurry into my bedroom and perch on the edge of my bed, lowering my head between my knees. Okay, Lexi, you need to calm the fuck down. Hyperventilating and passing out wouldn't be good. And isn't this putting the cart way before the horse? I don't know the depth of his feelings for me, other than that he enjoys fucking me and we have fun together.

Lying back on the bed, I meditate for a couple of minutes to clear my mind. When the stress drains from me, I can't help but laugh at myself. Jesus, I need to get a grip. Enjoy tonight and stop worrying about the future. I'm going to be the best breeding fucktoy there is! I snort and gingerly stand up, making sure I'm not still dizzy.

I've got a long day ahead of me: first work, and then when I get home I want to take a quick shower. I'll be a clean fucktoy until he gets me dirty again. My phone chimes loudly from the bathroom. Oh fuck, is that my warning alarm? I'm not sure where my morning went, but I guess the sooner I get to the pharmacy, the sooner Noah's cum will be inside me.

I daydream for a minute, remembering how wonderful it was last month when he came inside me. Mmm...and I get that again and again because he'll stay a couple nights with me. Last month it was the weekend, which was better, but he'll have to fuck me around my work schedule this time. It won't be a hardship to get a good boning before and after work for the next couple of days, and I'll hide my grin if any coworkers comment I seem chipper.

Wait, fuck, I need to stop wool-gathering. I laugh again. My smile never fades the entire time I'm rushing around getting ready.

CHAPTER
Eleven

When I get home, I have time to eat a sandwich and take a shower. Afterwards, I slip on a short cotton nightgown and panties. I'm halfway through blow drying my hair when I look up and see Noah's face behind me in the mirror. I yelp and nearly drop the dryer. He must have used his key to let himself in, and I didn't hear.

He grins and looks all innocent, as if he didn't know exactly what he did. "Hi."

Once the shock fades, a lightness enters my chest and my pulse speeds up. Knowing he was coming over tonight with the purpose of trying to get me pregnant makes it feel like we're in this together. The sense of shared purpose is nicer than I expected, even if I know he's only doing this for me.

Switching off the blow dryer, I set it down and give him a brief, but deep, kiss. "Hey, you."

He moves all the way into the bathroom and presses me back against the vanity. When I bump against it, he lifts me up and sets me on the counter. Oh, wow. A tingling sensation zips through me, straight to my pussy. Is he going to fuck me right here? I was a wet mess all day as I thought about tonight, but the shower got me nice and clean. My body is responding to Noah, and I feel myself becoming aroused again.

Standing between my legs, he kisses me with purpose, rolling his tongue with mine. A hum of pleasure lights my core. I'm needy for his cock, but I wouldn't mind a little teasing tonight. He could press his shaft against me through his clothes and drive me wild.

He's wearing jeans and a gray t-shirt. I notice he's barefoot, so he must have removed his shoes and socks when he got here. I run my hands up his chest and caress his neck, fiddling with the collar of his shirt while my fingers graze his neck. I've learned he has a sensitive neck, so I always touch or stroke it when I can.

I wish we were both naked and he was pressing into me right here. Why isn't he trying for more? He's standing between my legs with only my cotton panties and his jeans between him and my pussy, and he's not even trying to touch me there yet. He knew I would be ready for him as soon as he walked in the door. I want a tease, but not too much of one. I'm eager to get to the fucking. I could reach my hand down, unzip his pants, and he could push my panties to the side and slide in. Mmm, yeah.

My brain goes fuzzy as he keeps kissing me, and when he cups my breasts with both hands, I'm entirely in this moment. He flicks his thumbs across my hard nipples through the fabric of my nightgown, and I moan softly. My clit throbs in time with his caresses on the stiff peaks. I'm aching, and I want more than kisses and his hands on me.

"Oooh, god, that feels so good." I wrap my legs around him, drawing him closer. If he'd rub his hardness against me, maybe I'd get enough satisfaction to hold off the main course a little longer.

He stops kissing me and moves a hand up to my face to brush against my cheek. I'm flushed and desperate for his cock. Can't he see how much I need him? I gaze up at him, expecting him to turn into the hard dom I know he is and call me a breeding fucktoy.

He kisses my forehead. "Have you eaten dinner?"

I almost laugh. Food is the furthest thing from my mind at the moment. "Yes. I made a sandwich after work."

"Good girl." He leans down and gives me a featherlight kiss. A tingle runs down my spine and I wait, expectantly, for him to deepen the kiss and really go for it.

He doesn't.

His voice is husky when he murmurs against my lips. "Let's move to the bedroom."

He doesn't have to tell me twice. My pussy hums her approval while I unhook my legs to free him. I sort of wish he would carry me like he normally does, but I guess I can walk to the bedroom myself if his cock is the reward when we get there.

I slide off the counter and head straight to the bed. Before climbing on it, I make a move to strip off my nightgown, barely lifting it an inch before he makes me pause.

"Stop. Don't take it off."

My pussy tingles from him commanding me, and I lower the edge of the nightgown while I await his next instruction. I've always considered myself a strong woman. The sexual thrill I get from him taking control isn't anything I expected, though tonight, none of this is going as I thought it would. I assumed I was going to get wild, passionate Noah, but I don't see any evidence of him yet. Maybe he's warming up.

He holds my hand to his mouth and kisses my palm and then the pads of each finger. An unexpected zing of desire ripples through me, and I sway towards him. Why is this so hot?

Picking up the other hand, he kisses it the same way. Both my hands are up in the air while he entwines his fingers in mine.

"Lexi, we have a few rules tonight."

Yes, here we go! I shift and rub my thighs together in anticipation while my panties get more wet. I stare into his gorgeous eyes, and I'm lost for a moment, imagining how hard he's going to fuck me after he tells me the rules.

"First rule. You can't come without permission."

I nod. That seems standard for him, and I'm prepared to beg like a proper slut when the time comes.

"Second rule. I decide how I'm going to fuck you tonight, not you."

My lips part, and I'm about to complain, but I shut my mouth quickly. I mean, let's be honest here. He always decides, and I just beg. There's no point in arguing for something that won't happen, anyway. I nod again.

"Last rule. Tonight, you aren't my breeding fucktoy. Instead, you're my fertile goddess, and I'm going to worship every inch of you."

My heart races, and I lose all ability to think. A surge of passion courses through me when he holds me close. His arms wrap firmly around my waist, and he presses delicate kisses onto my neck.

Nibbling his way up, he pauses by my ear and whispers, "Don't worry, I'm still going to make you a beautiful mess. You'll be dripping with my cum and pregnant when I'm done with you."

Ohhh, hell yeah.

Noah slides his hands under my nightgown and helps me remove it. He kisses me passionately and wraps one hand around my neck, his thumb resting on my pulse point. As our tongues dance, my heart flutters. I bet he can feel my fast pulse.

I don't want to stay still while he thrills me, so I lift his shirt a little and run my fingers over his stomach and abs. I explore his warm skin as the kiss intensifies even more. There's a fire in my belly and I'm aching for him to fuck me, but he's in no hurry.

When he breaks off the kiss and nibbles down my neck, I moan softly as my needy pussy hums with pleasure. Running my fingers through his hair, I notice it's slightly damp, as if he recently took a shower. He must have stopped off at home after work. That means we're both clean and can make each other dirty.

He kisses between my collarbones, and further down my chest, stopping to suck on each nipple. I moan as he explores my plush globes with his hands, as if he's never touched them before. He teases my nipples with his tongue, sending tendrils of pleasure straight into my pussy. God, this is so amazing, but I'm desperate for his cock. My pussy clenches at the thought of him sliding inside me, and I'm enjoying the delicious torture of waiting. When he first enters me, it's going to be all that much sweeter after this extended foreplay.

He licks down my belly, swirling his tongue and giving me gentle kisses. He pays extra attention to the soft curve of my stomach that will swell once I'm pregnant. Imagining him kissing my pregnant belly in a few months makes me dizzy with need. I want it so damn much.

He hooks his fingers in the sides of my panties and drags them down as he kneels in front of me. I step out of them. He uses his hands to spread my pussy lips open and leans forward to taste me. Oh, fuck, that's good. Sharp spikes of bliss spiral through me, and I press my hands against his head and arch against him to help him get his tongue inside me further. I gasp when he laves my clit faster. A gush of wetness leaks out that he licks up. The longer he's between my legs, the closer I get to coming, and my toes curl on the rug while my body tenses. Each brush of his tongue against my sweet spot shoots pleasure through me, and I can't hold in my gasps and moans.

He pulls back, and I almost cry out in protest but hold it in. I can be patient and wait...for now.

He kisses the landing strip of soft curls before working his way back up. When he gets to my stomach again, he hums against my tummy and I giggle.

"I can't wait to see your belly grow with my child," he murmurs against my skin as he continues to lick until he's at my breasts.

Holy shit. The room tilts, and I close my eyes and repeat what he said to me in my head. My heart warms at the thought of us snuggling in bed while I'm eight months pregnant and huge. This is what I want more than anything.

When he's back up to my nipples, his mouth is a little more insistent, and I can tell he's wanting more. Maybe now I'll get that rough fucking.

He doesn't stay long at my breasts. When he stands and kisses me thoroughly, I can taste myself on him. A dirty thrill runs through me. When he breaks the kiss, I open my eyes and gaze at him through a cloud of lust. Fuck, he's good. I can't think of anything but him fucking and breeding me.

He smiles down at me softly and brushes his thumb across my cheek. "What do you want from me, Lexi?"

Thinking back to the first day when he demanded I tell him exactly what I wanted, I use my most seductive voice and tell him the same thing I said then. "Noah, I want you to fuck me and get me pregnant."

He pushes me backwards until my legs touch the side of the bed and grins. "What my goddess wants is what my goddess gets. Now get up on the bed in the center. I want you to close your eyes and think of how full your belly will be when I'm done with you."

Jesus Christ, this is hot. I understand how breeding kinks work since I have one, and there are different ways to do it. What he's saying to me tonight isn't how he was talking the other nights. It's blowing my mind because I don't know what to expect, and the affectionate way he's talking about breeding me is hitting me super hard now.

I crawl onto the bed, putting an extra wiggle into my ass in case he's watching. I can hear his jeans rustling, so I assume he's taking them off. When I roll onto my back, I prop up on my elbows to finish watching him strip. A hum of desire lights my core as I watch him. His shirt is already off, so he must have removed it while I was shaking my ass at him. He bends down to pick his pants and shirt off the floor, folds them, and sets them on my nightstand while I admire the ripple of his muscles.

When he turns towards me, I bend my knees slightly and spread my legs wide to expose my pussy and purr. "Come here and fill your goddess with your seed. My womb is begging for your cum."

I half expect him to laugh because what we're saying sounds ridiculous, but the dirty talk is turning me on even more. I'm embracing the silliness. Having the freedom to say whatever pops into my head is awesome and helps lighten the mood. All the months before Noah weren't anywhere near as much fun. They were miserable, and I wanted the dude to give me his cum and leave. Everything is so different with Noah, and I love that about him.

As he crawls between my legs, he growls and nips at my inner thighs, causing me to laugh. He pauses above my pussy, and his warm breath tickles me. I close my eyes, moaning and arching my back, hoping he'll give me a quick lick before fucking me.

"Lexi?"

I glance down and he's gazing into my eyes.

"Is my goddess ready to beg for her cum?"

"Mmm...I'm ready." I moan and arch my back, still hoping he'll give my pussy a quick lick.

He tastes me with a fluttering of his tongue against my clit, and I gasp from the ripple of delight. If I didn't want his cum so badly, I might have pleaded for more, but I really need his cock inside of me. He lingers there for only a moment and then nibbles up my belly. His tenderness is turning me on more than I expected, and my pussy aches for his hardness.

When his finger slips between my folds and brushes against my clit, I feel like I'm going to lose my mind. I gasp, "Ooooh, fuck. I need you, please?"

His mouth reaches my breasts and gives each soft globe a kiss. "Please, what? What does my goddess need?" he asks, and then sucks on a nipple, grazing it lightly with his teeth while rubbing tiny circles around my clit with his finger.

Pleasure zings through me, and I have a difficult time forming my words. "Please," I beg. "I need you inside me, fucking me...filling me. I need your cum."

"Mmmm," he moans around my nipple. "You're so beautiful when you beg. How can I resist you?"

When he calls me beautiful, heat climbs my body into my face. Fuck, Noah drives me wild. This soft side is messing with my head. I want him to call me a fucktoy and breed me hard, but I also want him to continue praising me and calling me a goddess. The two sides war within me, and I moan while pressing my pussy against his hand.

His question sounds rhetorical, so I don't answer. I slide my fingers through his hair, enjoying how silky it is, and the myriad sensations running through my body threaten to overwhelm me. At this rate, I'm going to come a hell of a lot quicker than I expected.

Neediness wells up inside me, and words flow from my mouth without thought as I beg again. "Please, Noah...please fill my fertile womb with your seed."

Noah brings out a side of me I didn't know existed. Around him, I'm a cum-greedy, sluttier version of myself, unafraid to say any naughty thing that pops into my head. He makes me extra filthy, and I'm ready to say whatever he wants if it gets his cum deep inside me.

He gives a last tug on my nipple with his lips and removes his hand from my pussy. I mewl in protest and rock against him, desperate to be filled. I've never been this eager to fuck someone before. My body responds to him on a primal level that goes beyond wanting him to breed me. A powerful craving for him to own me washes over me. I want to be his, but I can't say it because I don't know how he'll respond. I struggle to keep the need hidden instead of bursting out, begging him to claim me.

He gets on his knees and repositions himself between my legs. I sigh as he rubs the head of his shaft up and down my wet slit.

"Is this what my goddess wants?"

I can't take much more of this. I close my eyes while wiggling against the tip of his cock, hoping he'll push in. "God, yes, please."

He nudges the head against my clit. "You'll do anything for my cum, won't you?"

Shit, he's driving me insane. "Yes," I gasp, thrashing my head and tilting my hips with the hopes it will make him accidentally slip in. When he stills all movement, I realize he stopped. Cracking my eyes open, I see he's staring at me with a tender expression.

His voice is thick with need. "Fuck, you're stunning."

I open my mouth and a small, "Oh," escapes while my mind drains of all thought. A tremor of desire runs through me. With a groan, he presses inside me gradually. Each exquisite inch of him massages my cave walls, and I moan with delight. He's got such a thick cock, I'm always surprised at how far he stretches me out. I'm not sure I'll ever get used to its girth, and I'm okay with that.

When he bottoms out, he pauses and leans forward, covering my body with his so he can kiss me. Wrapping my arms around his neck, I pull him closer to me and rock my hips while I throw myself into the kiss. Our tongues duel, and I moan into his mouth when he fucks me.

Except it doesn't feel like fucking.

Each stroke of his cock is deep but gentle, and he's making love to me. He stops kissing me and thrusts steadily. I wrap my legs around him, trying to draw him in deeper as tendrils of bliss run through me.

When I gaze into his eyes, the intimacy of the moment leaves me vulnerable and breathless. I rock my hips in rhythm with his movements, and hot waves build in my core as I reel towards ecstasy. My body tenses, and I want him to fuck me harder. I'm edging closer to my orgasm, but I'm not sure I can come like this. I need something to give me the final push.

He must sense I desire more because he kisses me tenderly and whispers, "What do you need?"

I know what I want to say, but I'm ashamed to ask for it because it hits too close to my true feelings. Instead, I whimper, "You know what I want."

He gives me a sudden, sharp thrust, and my eyes widen. "Lexi, I need to hear you say it."

I buck against him, trying to make him fuck me faster and hope he'll take the hint. I'm afraid of what I'll say if I speak.

He stills his movement. "Do you want me to stop?"

Oh, fuck. I shake my head no.

He presses his lips to my ear and whispers, "Just say it, and I'll fuck you as hard and fast as you want."

To emphasize his point, he does another powerful thrust, and I cry out from the intense pleasure. Fuuuuuck. I unwind my legs from around him, putting my feet on the bed so I can get better leverage to arch against him. I move my hands to my breasts to play with my nipples, getting more desperate by the second.

"Say it, Lexi. Tell me what you want," he commands and slams into my pussy again.

A sharp jolt of pleasure makes my head spin and I blurt out, "I want you to fill me, claim me, and make me yours."

He pauses for a fraction of a second. "Oh, yeah?"

Not waiting for me to answer, he hammers into my pussy.

"Ohhh, God," I moan as my muscles tense and my thighs quiver. His reaction frees my inhibitions and my shame for wanting to be claimed drains away.

"Tell me who owns this pussy," he demands as he drills into me.

His words create an inferno in my core, and I can't stop the growing tsunami of pleasure. I whimper, "You do. You own this pussy."

He groans and picks up the tempo, slamming into me over and over, and pants, "Then how about I breed this pretty pussy of mine?"

God, I love the dirty talk and I almost come from how filthy we sound. "Yes, please, put a baby inside me."

He grunts as he drills into me. "Ask for it. Ask for my cum."

Fuck...my pussy throbs and tightens around him. I'm breathing hard and straining against him, so close to my orgasm. "May I have your cum, please, Noah?" I beg. "Please fill me up. Come inside me. I want to carry your baby."

My words spur him on, and the sound of wet slaps fills the room along with our moans.

"Look at me, Lexi."

It's hard to focus, but I meet his gaze.

"I'm going to come and mark you as my own."

He thrusts deep and hard.

I get a sharp thrill and breathe out, "Yes, do it. Make me yours."

"I'm going to put a baby in you."

He punctuates each sentence by slamming against my pussy while the pressure in my core builds to the breaking point.

"I'm going to make you pregnant, and all you have to do to get it is come for me."

Ohhh, fuck, that's hot. He slips a hand between us and brushes his finger against my clit while my pussy quivers. I'm so close to coming, and nothing is going to stop me.

He gives another hard thrust and growls, "Now come for me."

My orgasm rips through me, and I scream, bucking against him, as waves of bliss run from my fingers to my toes. He groans and slams into me one last time and blows his load. Spurt after spurt of his warm cum paints my cave walls, and his cock pulses and jerks while he fills me with his seed, claiming my pussy and womb.

Thinking we're done, I'm surprised when he fucks me slowly through the aftershocks of my orgasm. After a few moments, I'm sensitive and moan at the almost painful pleasure, which signals him to stop. When he withdraws, our combined juices drip out of me. I have the urge to keep his cum inside me somehow, but I know it doesn't matter. He gave me enough of his seed to knock me up if it's going to happen.

He stretches out next to me, and I roll onto my side to face him. We're both sweaty and panting softly. He plays with my hand, lost in thought, and twines his fingers with mine. A content drowsiness steals over me. I'm not sure how to take what just happened, but I feel so fucking fabulous. I want to enjoy the moment. I'll mull over what this all means—if it even means anything—later.

Snuggling closer to him, I nuzzle his chest, and he wraps his arms around me. Kissing my forehead, he murmurs, "You're so pretty when you come."

Despite being fully satisfied, a thrill zips through me. Fuck, why am I responding to his words like this?

Noah kisses my forehead again, and I sigh, relaxing against him. I want to stay in this bubble of happiness for as long as I can, so I let all thoughts drift away.

I wake up before Noah the next morning, and I make quick work of my morning routine. While I take a shower, I envision an idealistic future with Noah and a giggling baby. I could see it happening. The intimacy and connection between us last night was beyond my expectations. I'm not sure what to think. Did he experience it too? It really seemed like we were making love. If he felt nothing, wouldn't it have been more like all the other times? God, I hope it wasn't just me.

Since I didn't bring any clothes into the bathroom with me, I towel dry and sneak back into my room. The plan is to get something comfortable to wear before making breakfast. I stop being quiet when I see Noah is awake, naked, and sitting at the end of the bed. He blinks at me, still groggy, and gives me a tiny smile. He's so damn adorable with his tousled hair and sleepy eyes. I could gobble him up.

I grin at him. "Hey, you're awake. You hungry?"

As soon as I got the positive ovulation test yesterday, my brain blipped out, and I forgot to pre-plan meals for the days he'll be here. The best I can offer him is cereal or eggs. I'll run to the store after work and grab fresh fruit and muffins for a fast breakfast.

Moving between his legs, I bend down and give him a good morning peck on the lips. When I straighten up, he wraps his arms around my waist and hauls me towards him. He kisses my tummy and buries his head against me. A buzz of delight zings through me as I stroke his hair and stare off into space, forgetting about breakfast.

When did touching Noah become so natural? It's as if his body is an extension of mine. We've been seeing each other for such a short time I didn't notice when it started. It was the same way with Josh. I remember one day realizing that holding hands with him gave me a thrill, but it wasn't because his skin was different and new to me. It was comfortable and natural, like how Noah is in my arms right now.

When Noah places tiny, soft kisses on my belly, I melt against him while my pussy perks up. I sway against him and consider my options. I knew we were going to have sex again this morning, and I'm thinking breakfast can wait.

He pulls me down to the bed, and I yelp in surprise as I bounce against the mattress. He leans over me and attacks my neck, sending shivers down my spine.

Giggling, I push at him ineffectually. "Hey, what about breakfast?"

I don't really care about food, but I want to pretend. Maybe put up a little fight.

He kisses and sucks on the tender skin of my neck and growls. "You're going to be my breakfast."

Well shit, I can be down for this. My nipples harden, and my pussy aches with need. We don't have time for a long, drawn-out love fest, so he better not be a slow eater.

His hand skims down my belly with soft tickles and heads straight between my legs. When his fingers slip between my soft folds, I gasp as he rubs my clit. My pulse speeds up and I'm shocked at how fast I went from zero to sixty. I can tell I'm wet enough that his cock could slide right in without additional foreplay.

He sucks my earlobe and tugs on it with his lips. "Wait here a minute. I'll be right back."

I shudder when he gets off the bed. The lack of his warmth against me is noticeable as the cool air hits my body. Why does it seem like all men run at a higher temperature than women? I know I'm generalizing, but whenever I'm cold, having a guy around to warm my feet or hands is great...well, great for me. Maybe not so much for him.

While he's in the bathroom, I daydream about snuggling against him during the future winter months. He stretches out next to me when he returns. Leaning over me, he brushes his lips against mine, and I'm hit with a strong need to get him inside me immediately.

It's time to show him I'm not always submissive. He's mostly seen agreeable-me, but he should meet boss-me. Wrapping my arms around his neck, I kiss him soundly.

"Mmm...minty," I murmur against his mouth. He tastes like my toothpaste. The intimacy of him using my bathroom supplies gives me a jolt of satisfaction. Wanting to taste him, I deepen the kiss and coax his lips open.

We swirl our tongues together for a bit before he breaks off the kiss and nibbles down my neck. "So, where were we?"

His tiny bites at my neck send ripples of pleasure straight to my pussy, and I'm so turned on it's difficult to think. When he cups my breast with his warm hand and plays with my nipple, I moan as my desire builds.

No, that's not what we were doing. Maybe he needs a reminder. I capture the hand on my tit and move it down between my legs, spreading them open so he can touch me easily.

I purr at him. "This is where we were at." I press his hand against my pussy.

He slides a finger between my nether lips and strokes my clit. "Are you sure?"

"Yes," I gasp as delight builds in my core. I can tell it won't take me long to come today, which is good since we are about to be late for work and we can't stay in bed all day...making love over and over...and over.

He slips two fingers into my wet pussy and finger fucks me for a moment. "Are you positive it wasn't here instead?"

Oh, fuck...he's in a teasing mood. I need to put a stop to this right now and show him I'm the director this morning.

I try to channel what I imagine a dominatrix would sound like: authoritative, but sexy. "Noah, I'm not waiting this morning. You're going to remove your hand and fuck me. I need your cum in me right now."

He pauses his finger fucking. It sounds like he's holding back a chuckle. "Then we have a problem, Lexi, because if you want my cum this morning, you're going to have to beg for it again first."

Jesus Christ...him and his begging. Even as I mentally grouse, a thrill runs from my head to my toes, but I refuse to give in so easily.

He nibbles on my neck some more. I open my mouth to tell him I'm not begging when he whispers, "Just beg for it. I'll fill that pretty little pussy of yours with so much cum, you'll feel it dripping out of you all day."

Oh, fuck.

I melt against him and give in. I'll do or say whatever he wants if it gets me a pussy full of his cum faster. Taking a breath, I open my mouth to beg, but he stops me.

"Wait."

I'm floating in a fog of lust and confusion. Didn't he tell me to beg?

Before I can question him, he continues. "I haven't had my breakfast yet."

Ohhh, right. His moist kisses trail down my stomach. The closer he gets to my pussy, the more turned on I get. Shit, I was already willing to beg. His mouth against my sensitive parts will be delicious torture. He climbs between my legs while I bend my knees and get comfortable. Noah's been between my legs often enough that I've lost all inhibitions with him.

His mouth hovers over my slit, and his warm breath tickles the delicate skin. "Lexi, ask me to lick you."

Ugh, we've both learned that making me ask or beg turns me on even more. I'm not sure if I was always like this or if it's a response to him, but it drives me wild.

Attempting to focus, I smile at him. "Will you please lick my pussy... pretty please?"

I'd never asked anyone to do it before him. It was always a situation where if the guy went down on me, I didn't complain, but I only wanted it if the guy enjoyed it as well. Noah clearly is the type of guy who gets off on oral sex and relishes my reactions.

He traces my slit with his fingers and then uses both his thumbs to separate my folds, opening me up for his greedy mouth. As soon as his seeking tongue touches my clit, spikes of delight rush through my core.

Closing my eyes, I clutch the bedsheets and moan as he circles my bundle of nerves and alternates the swirls with licks from the flat side of his tongue.

Holy fuck. Digging my heels into the bed, I push my hips up, grinding my pussy against his face. It's vulgar, forcing my wetness on him, but he attacks my clit and pussy with gusto. Each swipe of his tongue sends ripples of delight through me. My thighs quiver as the pleasure mounts, and I gasp and moan with each lick. My last drops of desire to be in control dissipate, and I'm desperate for his cock.

His lips seal around my swollen clit, and the light suction zings pleasure through my pussy. My ass bucks off the bed as I almost come.

I can't take any more of this. "Oh god, Noah, will you fuck me and breed me, please?"

My words make him groan. It vibrates my clit, and a gush of wetness spurts from my pussy.

"Oh...my...god." I'm a needy mess, and bite down on my lips to muffle a scream when he slides his tongue into my slick cave.

I wasn't expecting him to go down on me this long, and the room spins as he fucks me with his tongue. Threading my fingers through his hair, I press his head to my pussy and arch against him as the spasms of delight build to the breaking point. The sensation is intense, and I'm on the brink of coming when he pulls back and crawls over me.

His lips brush against mine lightly, leaving a film of my juices. I taste myself as he deepens the kiss. Our tongues dance as he slides the underside of his cock along my wet slit. He's not pressing inside me, just teasing me with his hardness.

He breathes into my ear, tickling me. "Do you want me to fill you with cum?"

"Yes, please...fuck, yes. Fill me...breed me." I'm beyond thinking about what I'm saying, and I can only focus on his cock massaging my pussy.

"Before I do, I need you to know something." He moans softly and every part of me buzzes with excitement. He fits the head of his cock against my opening, parting my pussy lips, but doesn't press in. "Your pussy is mine. Say it."

"Ohhh fuck," I open my legs wider and whimper, "Yours...my pussy is yours."

"Mine," he growls and slams his cock into me.

I scream a stream of nonsense and buck against him as waves of rapture threaten to overwhelm me. He reaches down, rubs my clit, and I slip over the edge. Electricity races through me as he fucks me hard and fast, pounding into my pussy through my orgasm.

The pleasure seems never-ending, and his loud moans fill the room as his cock pulses. He comes with a shout, spurting his hot seed against my womb as he quivers with his release.

When he's done unloading, he rolls onto his side, taking me with him. We cuddle together as he wraps his arms around me. My heart is racing, and I melt against him as I come down from my orgasm.

He relaxes against me, our bodies slick with sweat, and I grin. "I'm going to need another shower."

"Mmm hmm," he mumbles, incapable of speaking actual words.

He's panting, and we both drift for a few minutes. This is my new happy place, and I don't want to move, despite knowing we need to get up and eat breakfast soon. Stupid bills that require us to work. Why can't we stay like this all day long?

"You're so perfect," he murmurs against my hair and kisses my forehead. A zing of happiness warms my heart, and I snuggle closer to him. This weekend is turning out better than I expected, and Noah's behavior has been an amazing mixture of loving and rough. If he wanted to call me his goddess more often, I totally wouldn't mind.

When his stomach growls, I giggle. "Why don't you shower, and I'll make us breakfast?"

"Sounds like a plan." He grumbles as we break apart, and I can tell he doesn't want to get up any more than I do.

My legs are rubbery from the orgasm, and I sit on the edge of the bed a moment to collect myself. My pussy feels used, and I get a slutty, dirty thrill when our combined wetness leaks out of me. He blows me a kiss and goes into the bathroom, and I stare off into space, daydreaming again about a baby in my arms.

Please, God, let me be pregnant.

CHAPTER
Thirteen

The following two days pass in a daze of work, sex, and more sex. Noah makes sure I'm so full of his cum that I have zero complaints when he kisses me goodbye. He's still planning to go on a trip and tells me he'll message me with details. I almost smile but stop myself in time. Of course he'll let me know, so I won't expect him to come over for our sex sessions.

Since I'm off work for a couple of days, I ditch my nightgown and crawl into bed after he leaves. Yawning, I contemplate the ceiling and rub my belly. I hope his swimmers from the attempt this morning are taking hold right now, if I'm not already pregnant from our previous rounds. I'm so dang tired. It was probably for the best that we had our marathon baby-making session on days we had to work. I'm going to need these days off to relax and recover.

Noah treated me differently from last month. He worshipped me like I was a precious vessel while still thrilling me with his roughness and forcing me to beg for his cum. I love being called a fucktoy and the degradation aspect of what he was doing last month. But being his goddess was equally amazing. I really don't know which way I prefer, but I hope I'm pregnant and won't have to find out what he'll do next month. Since this is only our second month trying, I know the odds aren't in our favor, but I'm so close to having everything I want, I can practically taste it.

My pussy buzzes and a soft tingle of pleasure swirls in my belly as I cup my breasts gently and play with my nipples. I'm still wet and full from him. It's hard to tell if my increased wetness is because I'm thinking of him or if I'm still sensitive from our playful romp in the sheets an hour ago.

Bending my knees, I spread them and trail a hand down between my legs. Mmm, I'm still soaking. Knowing the wetness is our combined juices is erotic as all fuck. I caress my clit, imagining it's his hand doing it for a few moments while a soft pleasure builds. Moving my wet fingers up to my breast, I tug and pull at my nipple and imagine my breasts are sensitive because I'm pregnant. I massage the sticky wetness from my pussy into my nipple, and a tingle runs through my body as I think about how filthy the last few days were.

I push aside any worry about rubbing his cum into my skin since I need a shower, anyway. I could paint my entire body with his cum, and it wouldn't matter. Rubbing his seed into my nipples gives me a delicious naughty zing. As the pleasure builds in my core, I consider going to town and giving myself another orgasm, but I need a nap.

Forcing myself to stop touching my breasts, I contemplate the ceiling again while a fuzzy contentment washes over me. It's hard to imagine how life could get much better than it is right now, since everything is falling into place. It's been several shitty years, and I finally have hope for the future again.

Noah fucked me good and hard, and I had more orgasms than I can count. I'm going to be thinking about him for days. It wasn't the fantastic sex that blew my mind. Noah makes me feel safe, and for the first time in a very long time, I feel as if I'm not alone in the world...as if I have a partner and a purpose.

Ever since I lost Josh, I've felt like half of me was missing. Nothing mattered, and I was adrift with no anchor. I don't want a child to complete my life or make me whole again, but to matter to someone and feel connected. Being with Noah shows me how much I'm missing. It's corny, but I feel alive again.

When an enormous yawn breaks my train of thought, I softly smile at nothing and force myself to close my eyes. I really need to get some sleep and then take a shower because I'm dirty. I giggle...yeah, my body and my thoughts are both unclean.

I take a while to fall asleep, so I don't know how long I napped, but when I wake up, it's midafternoon, and I'm hungry. A surge of energy runs through me, and I practically jump out of bed with excitement. I thought I'd be groggy, but I'm invigorated and ready to seize the day.

Bouncing into the kitchen, I'm on cloud nine while I make a sandwich and daydream about a future adorable baby with Noah's eyelashes. I know I shouldn't get my heart set on any child of ours having his eyelashes, but I allow myself this fantasy. Dreaming is fun, and as long as I know it's not a done deal, it's okay. I don't look at it any differently from a daydream about winning the lottery. It could happen, though chances of having a baby with his eyelashes are probably better odds than winning the lotto. There's no harm in a little fanciful dreaming now and again.

My phone vibrates with an incoming text message.

NOAH

> I've been thinking about you. Work is busy today, but I'll text you when I get home.

Smiling softly, I text him back.

LEXI

> I've been thinking of you too. Don't work too hard, and I'll talk to you later.

God, he's so thoughtful. He always tries to let me know when he's busy or won't be around. If I could only get him to show up on time for dates, then he'd be perfect.

My sandwich is extra tasty today. I enjoy a soft breeze coming through my open window and the warmth of the sun as I sit at my kitchen table. Why doesn't Noah think he's good in a relationship? Everything he does tells me otherwise. After worshiping me during sex, I really think he loves me even if he hasn't said it.

I daydream some more while I finish my sandwich and contemplate what I want to do today and tomorrow. The last few days were a whirl-wind of excitement, and I didn't plan my days off. I don't have any errands that desperately need taking care of. Since I just saw a ton of Noah, he probably isn't coming over. I'm a free woman for a change, and I don't know what to do with myself.

After I'm done eating, I make a cup of chai tea and wander into the living room. I stop in front of the fireplace mantle. I look at the pictures and mementos of Josh. Maybe it's time to put some of this away? A gentle, happy squeezing around my heart as I think of my future tells me I'm ready.

I spend most of the day going through my condo and boxing up stuff for donation. It's interesting how many little things I kept of Josh's that I would never use, but couldn't bring myself to pack away. I hesitate when I find his tool belt, remembering all the sexy jokes we shared whenever he had it on and was fixing something. I'm not the handy type and would hire someone to fix most things. Sighing, I add it to the box to donate. There are a few items I'm keeping, but the tool belt won't be one of them.

His clothes are the biggest hurdle since they're still in my closet, taking up a third of the space. Each item brings back memories of a time he wore it, and brief flashes of pain stab me every time I set aside a piece that has a memory attached to it. I hug a couple of his shirts before adding them to the pile. The absence of Josh's smell hurts. They've been in the closet for three years, so other than being slightly musty, all traces of his scent are gone.

By the end I'm in tears, but looking at the empty space also brings me comfort. The fact I'm not curled up in a ball on my bed, sobbing, speaks volumes about the progress I've made. I probably could have done this sooner, but I'm glad I waited until I felt ready.

There were a couple of clothing items I couldn't donate: my favorite sweater of his and his high school letterman's jacket. I pack both of them with the trinkets and framed pictures I'm keeping and slide the box into the top shelf of my storage closet. Everything else gets piled into my car. The clothes alone take up most of the trunk. I'm hot and sweaty by the time the car is loaded, but I want to get it all done today, so I make the short trip to the donation station.

When I get home, I take a long shower to wash off the layer of dust clinging to me. I'm tired and emotionally drained, but the warm water soothes me and a weight lifts from my shoulders. Those things aren't Josh, and the memories of him are still with me. I'm ready to embrace the new chapter of my life.

Putting on clean panties and a fresh nightgown, I rub my stomach and smile softly. Hopefully, I'm pregnant and Noah is part of my future. I pick up my phone and head to the kitchen to make hot chocolate and figure out what I'm doing for dinner. It might be a pizza delivery night. I haven't ordered in a while, and curling up on the couch to watch a mindless rom-com and scarfing down pizza sounds like the perfect evening. I could invite Noah over and tell him it's only for pizza and not sex.

I giggle at myself. When I pull up the app to order, I see Noah messaged me while I was in the shower.

NOAH

> Hey, I could catch a flight out tonight and I'm packing now. I'll call you tomorrow when I get settled in. Thank you for a wonderful time.

Boo, no pizza night for him. I message him back and wish him a pleasant flight. For a moment, I'm disappointed he's leaving tonight, but quickly brighten. This way I get to choose the movie and can get jalapenos on my pizza without worrying about what he wants. He and I haven't had the jalapeno discussion, and he better either be fine with jalapenos or at least okay if one touches his side. Some of my friends claim they can't even have them on the same pizza at all because it taints their half, and I don't want to order two pizzas for the rest of my life. Plus, this gets his trip out of the way and he'll be home sooner. I'd like him to be back by the time I take another pregnancy test. The way he helped me the first month was incredibly thoughtful, and I might need his strength again this month.

By the time the pizza arrives, I've chosen a movie and a potential second one. I'm ready for a marathon and to stuff myself so full of pizza

I can't move. As I press play, I snuggle in. A warm contentment washes over me.

Today might have been difficult emotionally, but I feel better than I have in a very long time. The future excites me, and I found someone worth loving again. As the saying goes, "The only way out is through." I might be through the super shitty time of my life at last.

CHAPTER

Fourteen

The next day, Noah calls me early in the morning and wakes me up. We have a very brief conversation while I'm groggy, and I immediately fall back asleep after we disconnect. When I wake again, I don't remember everything we talked about. Did he tell me where he went? I don't think he did. Shit, why is he being so secretive about this trip?

Grumbling, I get out of bed and face the prospect of another day off with nothing I need to do. After my shower, I open my closet to get clothes out and freeze. My eyes widen while my skin tingles and tightens with discomfort. I stare at the space where Josh's clothes used to be for a moment. Fuck, how long will it take me to get used to this?

I wander aimlessly around my condo, noticing all the now-empty surfaces. It didn't seem like I donated that much stuff, but I'm disconcerted whenever I see something is missing. A heaviness settles in my stomach, and I consider calling Kylie, the one friend I still have.

After Josh passed, I stopped talking to most of our friends because it hurt too much. I disliked having to lie and tell everyone I was doing okay. Looking back, I don't know why I felt I had to be dishonest. No one expected me to be fine, but everyone experiences grief differently. After a year of shittiness, I felt guilty whenever I wanted to talk about my problems. I wove stories in my head that weren't based on reality. I told myself people were sick of me whining about my husband dying, despite no one ever actually saying that to me.

After I got some therapy, I understood more about the process of grief, but I never contacted my other friends again. They were our shared friends, and it was a different time in my life. I wanted to move on. Except for Kylie. She was always there for me. If I didn't call or text her, she'd contact me. She didn't let me hide from her. She checked up on me when I wasn't communicating. It brought us closer together, for which I'm grateful. She knows I'm seeing someone casually, but doesn't know his name, and I'm not ready to admit to anyone that I'm in love again. I've been avoiding her for a few weeks now.

I putter around, cleaning and rearranging knickknacks to reclaim the bare surfaces. My leftover pizza reheats nicely in the air fryer. After my tasty dinner, I relax and read until bedtime. While I'm still uneasy about the changes I made, I'm breathing easier. A lightness enters my chest as I snuggle into bed and pull the comforter up to my chin. Noah didn't text today, but I still send him my usual goodnight text.

There isn't a text waiting for me in the morning, and after I message him to wish him a good day, I stay busy so I can ignore my phone. My work-week starts, and I'm well-rested from two nights of good sleep after the fuck-fest with Noah. I'm chirpy and flit around work making everyone laugh, but every time I check my phone and there isn't a text from Noah, I get more tense. By the time work ends, I'm subdued. When I go to bed that night. I send him another goodnight text, but as soon as I do, I wonder if it was a mistake. Why isn't he responding? A pit opens up in my stomach and it's difficult to sleep.

I don't text him when I wake up, and a third day goes by without him contacting me. By the time I get home from work, I'm vacillating between irritated and concerned. I don't want to contemplate any thoughts of an accident, so I focus on the idea he's not contacting me because he doesn't want to. His lack of response is annoying, and I wish he'd just text me.

The real problem is, of course, that he's not obligated to contact me at all. We aren't officially dating and he made no promises. This high-lights the fact we don't have any commitment beyond fucking. I never told him I enjoy our good night and good morning texts. We just fell into the habit. I didn't realize how much I depended on them, and how addicted I was to the jolts of excitement I got whenever he messaged me.

I still can't get over the surprise of seeing Josh's stuff gone, and it's adding to my general unease regarding Noah. For all I know, Noah might have told me he wouldn't be in contact for a few days and I don't remember because I was only half awake. Should I message him again? No, I need to stop fawning over him. He'll contact me if he wants to.

By the time I go to bed, my muscles are tight and I'm on edge. Deep breathing exercises help me calm down. I didn't even want a relation-ship. Maybe I was right all along and don't need one. I've had a rough couple of days. My condo is weirding me out with how different it feels, on top of Noah's mysterious trip and lack of communication.

Everything will be better tomorrow. It has to be. I get bored with my deep breathing and curl up on my side. Staring at the wall in the dark-ness, I wait for sleep to claim me.

Why couldn't he have just texted me?

~

On the fourth day of Noah's trip, I wake to a text from him. I can't help the zing of delight that runs through me, and I'm instantly wide awake from a rush of adrenaline.

NOAH

Hey, I'll be back on Friday morning. If you're free that night, I could come over.

I want to put off responding so he doesn't see how much angst I've had through the last few days, but I immediately text back.

LEXI

Yep, sounds good.

He could have at least said he missed me, or apologized for not responding to me for days. I probably shouldn't have been so fast with agreeing to see him. But he wants to come over the day he gets back, so that has to mean something, even if he isn't saying the words I want to hear.

NOAH

I'll be there around 8:30.

Why does he sound so cold? He's not helping ease the anxiety I've been living with since he left. I give him a simple reply.

LEXI

Okay, I'll see you then.

After I send my message, I set my phone on my nightstand and stare at the ceiling. Mixed emotions tumble through me, and I'm not sure whether to let myself be happy or if I should still be upset that he ignored me for days.

Grumbling to myself, I get out of bed and start my morning. It can't be Friday fast enough.

Fifteen

Despite thinking the days would go slowly, I blink and it's Friday. I take a half day from work, so when Noah gets here I'm showered and wearing my favorite cotton nightgown and no underwear. As soon as I hear his key in the door, my heart pounds and my stomach clenches. I made sure I was on the couch in the living room so I could watch the door and greet him as soon as he walks in. A quick glance at my phone tells me he's only five minutes late tonight, and I hold in my smile. That's prompt for him. Was he in a hurry to get here?

He halts as soon as he sees me, and a smile blossoms on his face. "Hi."

I want to stay annoyed, so I fight the urge to jump up, throw myself into his arms, and kiss him all over his face. Forcing myself to stay on the couch, I watch him with cool eyes. I try to hide my delight from being in the same room with him again.

As he sets his overnight bag down, I can tell he's tired by how slowly he's moving and the slight slump to his shoulders. My sympathetic side kicks in, and the ball of anxiety I've had in my gut for days eases. He could have been at home asleep, but he wanted to see me instead. All the vague ideas I had about confronting him slip away. Tonight isn't the time for deep conversations. I'll ask him another day why he ignored my messages.

I hold my arms out to him. "Come here and snuggle."

He kicks off his shoes before joining me on the couch. He's wearing sweatpants and a t-shirt, so he came over with comfort in mind. I expect him to sit next to me. When he puts a knee on the cushion and pulls me against him for a deep kiss, my head whirls before I allow myself to relax and enjoy the moment.

"Mmmmm," I murmur against his mouth when I taste peppermint. My arms wrap around his neck as he presses my back to the couch. I wasn't in the best position for this, so I break the kiss and adjust my body underneath his, accidentally knocking our heads together.

"Ouch," we both exclaim in unison, and I giggle.

He rubs his forehead and then leans into me and kisses the spot on my head where we bumped.

"There, now you'll feel better."

A pleasant warmth runs over me, and I smile. "Yep, all better."

Shit, does he have to be so sweet all the time? Since I've stopped squirming, he covers me with his body but supports his weight with his arms. Spreading my legs, I make room for him to fit against me, and his hardness presses me through his sweatpants, making my pussy tingle.

I guess someone isn't too tired tonight. He kisses me thoroughly again, and pings of bliss ripple through my body as our tongues play together and he dry humps me. God, I missed this. We haven't gone this long without sex for a couple of months, and I got used to getting cock on the regular.

Arching my back, I try to force him to rub against me faster. I'm aching, and the friction is enough that I might come if he would press down a little harder. He stops kissing me and nibbles down the column of my neck, and I slide my hands behind his head and play with his hair.

"Mmmm. You feel good," I whisper as he licks and sucks gently on the tender skin around the collar of my nightgown.

He growls, "I've been thinking of fucking you all day," and I moan. His cock is going to feel so damn wonderful with that first thrust inside me.

I'm tingling wherever the rough bristles of his five o'clock shadow touch me, noticing every movement. When he runs a hand down between us and pushes my nightgown up, he hums approval at my bare, wet pussy.

"Looks like my fucktoy is ready to be played with."

As soon as he calls me his fucktoy, my brain empties of everything but the desire to get his cock inside me. When he slips his fingers between my wet folds and brushes against my clit, the spikes of bliss radiate through my core.

I groan, "Oh god, fuck me, please. I need your cock. It's been too long."

He chuckles against my neck but doesn't respond. I want to feel his bare skin against mine, so I run my hands down his sides and try to tug his shirt up. He takes the hint and helps me get his shirt off. Once he's bare chested, I caress his shoulder and down the front of him, enjoying how his muscles jump when I hit his sensitive spots.

I thought he'd go straight for my pussy again, but he tugs on my nightgown instead. I arch my back so the fabric isn't trapped underneath me. He slides it up and exposes my breasts. He buries his head between them, playing with my nipples, and I moan as soft pleasure zips through me straight to my pussy. When he pretends he's trying to devour them and pushes them together so he can motorboat them while we're lying down, I burst out in giggles. God, I love Noah's silly side.

"You goofball. Are you going to fuck me, or are you going to play with my boobs all night?"

He tilts his head up, and his eyes sparkle. All traces of his exhaustion have vanished. "That depends. Did you forget how to beg while I was gone?"

When he asks me if I'm going to beg, I glare at him with narrow eyes as a wave of crankiness hits me. Is this motherfucker going to make me beg every time we have sex? Even as I have the thought, my grumpiness fades. We both know I'm going to beg. I'll end up saying anything to get his cock. I might be addicted to it.

"Noah, you should know me by now. I'm going to beg as hard as you want and as much as you want. I'm going to be the best fucktoy there is."

He hums, "Mmmm, nice," and runs his hand between my legs. He dips his finger into my pussy to gather moisture and uses it to rub my clit again while my body lights up with pleasure.

"Such a sweet and wet fucktoy. I think I'm going to enjoy using you tonight."

My breath catches, and my heart pounds when he mentions using me. It's not my fertile time of the month and I'm hoping I'm already pregnant, but this means he can come wherever he wants. Fuck, I still really want it inside me. I love having a squishy, messy pussy so full of cum that it drips out of me.

When he slides a finger into me, I moan, "God, please fuck me."

"I don't think so," he chuckles. "That wasn't good enough begging for a fucktoy."

When a second finger joins his first, he massages my cave walls with both of them. The in-and-out movement shoots ripples of pleasure through my core. I rock my hips, trying to get him to fuck me faster while I run my hands along his shoulders and down his arms. I love how I can feel his strength and how it contrasts with my softness. He makes me feel small and vulnerable, and it excites me to know he can hold me down and take what he wants, even if he'd never hurt me.

His fingers in my pussy are making it difficult to think, but maybe two can play this game. I explore his body, paying close attention to the spots I know are sensitive. Whenever my hands brush his sides lightly, he shivers, so I run my fingers from his waistband all the way up his side. When my fingers travel back towards his legs, I can feel the goosebumps, and I grin. Gotcha. I caress his stomach softly, enjoying the roughness of his small patch of hair.

I only get to enjoy his belly for a moment before he growls and stops rubbing my pussy. He grabs both of my hands, pinning them to the couch cushion above my head. "That's enough of that. It's time for you to beg for my cock."

His voice has an edge to it, and I can tell it really is time for me to beg. He releases my wrists and one-handedly pulls his sweatpants down far enough to release his thick cock. Mmmm, oh god, I'm so close to getting that inside me. My pussy buzzes, and I'm willing to do whatever it takes to get him to fuck me.

I try to entice him with my sexiest voice. "Please, Noah, will you please, please, please, please use my pussy and fill me with your seed?"

He grasps the tip of his cock and runs it along my wet slit but doesn't press in. I nudge my pussy against him as I tingle from the anticipation of the first thrust.

When he says, "Try again," my head spins.

I arch my back, hoping he'll slip the head of his cock in, and gasp out, "Oh god, Noah, what do you want? I'll do anything for you...tell me what you want. You can call me whatever you want, I'll say whatever you want, I'll call you Master for the day, I'll be the best fucktoy there is for you. Please, please, please fuck me."

He stops all movement and leans over and kisses me deeply. He coaxes my mouth open, and as our tongues twirl together, I slip my arms around his neck and play with his hair. I'm beyond thinking of anything except his cock.

He breaks off the kiss and gives my nose a quick peck. "I like the sound of being called Master...now ask your Master to fuck you, and I will."

I flush, and my heart races. Since I'm so close to getting his cock, I don't hesitate. "Please, Master, please, will you fuck me?"

I expect him to ram his cock into me as soon as I ask, so when he slowly sinks between my folds, I groan from the intense bliss. Fuuuuck, how did I forget how thick he was? Pleasure ripples through my core as he stretches me out with his long stroke. When he's buried to the hilt, he immediately pulls out all the way and presses back in. My entire body sings while he fucks me like he's got all the time in the world.

The room tilts from the spikes of pleasure, and I grab the edges of the couch to hold on and enjoy the ride. Each stroke gets me closer to coming, and it doesn't take long before I'm moaning and writhing desperately.

If he would just speed up, I'd get there faster. I wrap my legs around his waist, hoping to force him to do what I want, but all it does is makes me needier. The new angle hits different nerve endings, and it drives me wild. I mewl in distress when he brings me right to the edge. My thighs tense and my pussy quivers. I can't handle this much pleasure, and I need to come.

Noah's voice is harsh. "Fucktoy, ask your Master if you can come."

As soon as he mentions me coming, I almost climax. I gasp, "Master, please can I come?"

Noah speeds up his thrusts. After a few strong whacks against my pussy, he growls out, "Come for me, my sweet little fucktoy."

Rapture zings through me as I explode around his cock. I close my eyes as colors burst behind my lids and scream out, "Ohhhh, god," as euphoria surges through me. My pussy quakes, and it tips him over the edge with me. He groans as he comes and buries his cock in me while he shoots load after load of his cum into my grasping, needy pussy. He flexes his buttocks and drills into me, fucking me, as we both shudder from our powerful climaxes.

When he slows down and relaxes against me, I'm glowing with deep satisfaction. He kisses the side of my neck and murmurs, "Fuck, I missed this."

I'm a jumble of emotions. I missed him, and his cock, but I want to say it in a light and teasing way. My brain isn't working, and I can't think of the words, so I give a soft, "Mmm hmm," in agreement. We float for a bit, and eventually he moves next to me on the couch and I roll to my side so we can spoon. A moment later, he's breathing heavily and if he's not already asleep, he's close to it.

We should get up and go to the bedroom, but that seems like too much work right now. My eyelids get heavy. I give up the fight and yawn loudly. It better have been more than just the sex he missed. I'll have to razz him about that in the morning.

CHAPTER
Sixteen

At some point in the night, we move to the bed. The next morning, Noah wakes me up with a gentle hand on my breast. I don't hold in my sigh of pleasure, and when he realizes I'm awake, he plays with my nipples. It turns into another round of thrillingly rough sex, and my head is spinning by the time we're done. When he gets up, I assume it's to use the bathroom, and then we'd either snuggle or make breakfast.

Instead, he smiles at me. "Hey, I'm sorry, but I need to run this morning. My condo is a mess since I've been gone all week, and I need to pick up Bandit from the kennel."

"Oh, okay." I try to keep the hurt out of my voice. I was hoping we could talk over a leisurely breakfast.

I try to sit up, but he motions for me to stay down. "I'm going to head straight out. Why don't you get some more sleep?"

I relax, and he walks around the bed to kiss my forehead, murmuring, "I'll text you later."

Pulling the comforter up to my chin, I snuggle as he heads towards the door. I call out, "Talk to you later. I had fun last night."

He looks at me over his shoulder and grins. "Yes, I did too."

"Yeah, see you," I grumble to myself as he walks out the door.

Once he's gone, I sigh and look at the ceiling. Dammit, I was hoping he would tell me where he went. It seems so odd that he didn't contact me for a few days. He also seemed less loving last night and this morning. I'm not sure how to take it. My stomach churns. Fuck, those few days that I was ovulating, the sex was so amazing. What is up with the change in him? Was I wrong, and he doesn't love me? My chest tightens. What if I imagined our connection?

I sit straight up at the next thought. What if he's got a fucking girlfriend? He said he didn't, but what do I really know about him? I flush with anger at the thought. Or maybe it's not a girlfriend, maybe she's a fuck buddy. What if those days he didn't contact me he was off impregnating another woman? Hell, maybe this is what he does.

When I realize my pulse is speeding up, I take a mental pause. Wait, I need to chill the fuck out and not mentally spiral about things I don't actually know. He and I agreed not to sleep with anyone else after we got the STD tests. Since he's the one who brought up testing, I doubt he'd break the rule. And there *is* a lot I still don't know about him, but deep down I know he's a good guy; he's just a private person.

The tension drains from my body, and I laugh at myself. Jesus, I need to stop obsessing about this damn trip of his. I'm sure whatever it was, it was innocent. He probably didn't think it was worth mentioning to me, or he told me the morning I was half awake and I don't remember.

The real problem is that I need to tell him how I feel. There wasn't much time between him fucking me stupid last night and then him leaving so quickly this morning. The rush made it difficult to open up. I should invite him over for a romantic dinner and admit my feelings. I'm not the world's greatest cook, but I can make a pretty damn good pork chop with mashed potatoes.

As I text Noah, I'm mentally preparing the meal. When I ask him if he wants to come over for dinner later, he replies sure and says he'll be there at seven. Excitement bubbles in my belly. Am I going to talk to him, or am I going to chicken out?

I'm in a dither for the rest of the day, and I'm glad it's my day off from work. A trip to the store in the afternoon kills some time. While I'm getting dinner supplies, my eyes light up when I spot chocolate cake sold by the thick slice. I grab a piece to share with him for dessert. Nothing says romance like chocolate cake in my book.

I hem and haw over what to wear tonight because I don't want to seem like I think this is a romantic date, but I also don't want it to be another normal night. Since it's warm outside, I choose my favorite pair of shorts that are tight over my ass and accentuate my curves. To add a touch of romance, I wear a flowing peasant top along with a silver teardrop necklace. The teardrop nestles perfectly in my cleavage, and a glance in the mirror tells me I'm looking sexy tonight. Perfect.

I'm a nervous wreck and almost done making dinner when Noah arrives. Since I'm busy at the stove, I don't hear him come through the front door.

I jump in surprise when he says, "Hey there, sexy," from the kitchen doorway.

He's dressed casually, like he usually is, in jeans and a t-shirt, but he's already removed his shoes. Shit, even his bare feet are sexy. A warmth runs through me at the thought that I have a man who's comfortable enough to let himself in and take his shoes off before he greets me. Yeah, I really need to talk to him.

He slides his hands around my waist and presses against me from behind. He kisses my neck and asks, "Can I help with anything?"

Melting in his arms, I moan, "Mmm, yes," and tilt my head in the opposite direction. "I think you missed a spot."

He pushes my hair aside so he can nibble the exposed column, and pleasure ripples down my back. Shit, why isn't dinner over and the tough part of the evening out of the way? I'm sure the anxiety will disappear once we talk. I wish I could relax and enjoy the moment, but I can't yet.

Regaining the moment, I swat him away and gesture towards the cupboard by the sink. "You can grab some glasses and get us something to drink while I finish cooking."

He gets us both some sparkling water from the fridge and takes it out to the dining room. When he comes back, he keeps me giggling with a running commentary of the shitty things he's seen at work over the years while I finish cooking and plate the food. Since he does a lot of divorce cases, he's seen some shady things go down. I should probably feel bad because going through a divorce sucks and can make people crazy, but it's difficult not to laugh when the stories are so damn ridiculous.

When we sit down and eat, he appreciates my meal, and I'm ecstatic that he likes it. If we end up together long term, he's going to be eating plenty of pork chops.

Throughout dinner, the conversation is light and flirty. It's fun, but I really need to talk to him before dessert. Chocolate cake will be more romantic after we both admit we're fond of each other beyond just friends.

There's a brief lull in the conversation, and I take the opportunity. "Noah, have you ever thought about what will happen after I get pregnant?"

He smiles at me, and his voice is casual. "I try not to worry about the future."

Okay, not quite what I was expecting. "Yeah, but I have grown pretty fond of you. I would hate to lose you as a friend."

He winks. "Well, that's because I'm awesome."

His face doesn't change, but he shifts in his chair as if he's uncomfortable. I'm slightly irritated because he's not making this easy. I need to just go for it.

"I'd be sad to see you go."

I sit expectantly while he's quiet for a moment. I hope he's going to repeat that he would be sad to see me go as well.

He sets his fork down before responding, and his voice is cautious. "I would enjoy staying in contact to see pictures of the child as they grow up. So we don't have to say goodbye."

I stare at him in shock, uncertain what to say, and my throat clogs.

Holy fuck, is he saying what I think he's saying?

Silence hangs in the air for a few moments, and I laugh casually to hide my discomfort. "Good, then we're on the same page. I was hoping we could be friends."

He toys with his silverware without looking up at me. "I'm glad we're having this conversation. I was afraid I was giving mixed signals."

He pauses, and my stomach hardens while my throat feels tight. My voice might croak if I speak, so I take a sip of water.

He continues before I have time to say anything. "I enjoy being a sperm donor for people who need help." He shrugs. "I don't know. I like the idea of helping families. But especially since I can't have one myself."

My pulse speeds up. This is such bullshit. I open my mouth to tell him exactly that, but he mutters, "I'm too fucked up from my childhood. I'd be a horrible father. Not that I want that, anyway."

My body is heavy as disappointment simmers inside me. I need to take what he says at face value. How many times has he told me he doesn't want a relationship? And yet I keep having hope. A kaleidoscope of emotions ripples through me. I don't want to examine them right now, so I try to push them aside.

Needing something to do, I stand up, grab my almost-empty plate and head to the kitchen, talking to him over my shoulder. "Well, you don't need to convince me. I was just checking to make sure we could stay friends."

He doesn't follow me, and I'm glad since I'm close to tears. I need that chocolate cake, but not for romance. I want to stuff my face and forget this dinner ever happened. Since I never actually told him I had bought dessert, I don't have to share. He may have seen it in the fridge before dinner, but since it's one slice, he wouldn't know I planned it for tonight. Yeah, fuck him. He doesn't deserve my romance cake. Now I need to get him out of here before I cry.

Noah calls from the dining room, "Hey, I'm beat. I'm going to head out for the night."

I can't help the tiny, "Oh, okay," that pops out.

"Do you want any help cleaning up?"

I try to sound cheerful. "No, I'm good."

Ugh, he's leaving. Even though this is what I want, my mind races and tries to think of any way to make everything better. I walk back to the entryway of the dining room, and he's standing up with his hands on the back of his chair like he just pushed it in. His face is unreadable. For a man who crushed some of my hopes and dreams, he looks pretty damn calm about it. My eyes burn as I try to hold back tears. He really needs to get the fuck out.

Trying to pretend nothing is wrong, I fix a smile on my face.

"Thanks for coming. I was craving pork chops, and it was my turn to cook for you."

He flashes me a grin that doesn't reach his eyes and walks over to kiss my forehead. "It was delicious. Thank you for having me over."

I give a nod and follow him to the front door. He slips his shoes on and steps close to me, and my breath catches, expecting a kiss. When he brushes his thumb across my cheek, I try to hide how upset I am by keeping my expression relaxed.

His voice is husky. "Have a good night, Lexi."

My heart aches as I hold the door open and whisper goodbye. After he leaves, I shut it and lock the deadbolt before leaning against the door. It's hard to catch my breath, and the panic wells up. The kitchen needs cleaning, but the damn dishes can wait.

Making a beeline for the couch, I slump into the cushions. I attempt my deep breathing exercises as tiny stabs of pain poke at my heart. I can't believe I thought he loved me. Why did I let myself get attached? I knew this was a bad idea. He told me at the beginning he was a flawed man and not good with relationships. Shit, I really thought he liked me—no, that he loved me.

A couple of tears roll down my cheeks, and I wipe them away. When more spill out, I surrender to self-pity. Sobbing, I bury my head into a pillow and let loose. God, why did I even put myself in this position? Even if I wanted a relationship, it wouldn't be with Noah. I don't want a guy with intimacy issues, and clearly, he has a lot. If I ever date, I want the guy to be all in from the beginning.

I let myself cry for a while. When the tears finally subside, I'm drained, but also refreshed. I'm just going to focus on myself and not worry about any future with Noah.

If I keep repeating this, maybe someday I might actually believe it.

CHAPTER
Seventeen

For the next couple of weeks Noah still comes over regularly, but something doesn't feel right. The sex is still amazing, and he definitely knows how to press every filthy button of mine fabulously, but there is no sign of Loving Noah. I keep telling myself it doesn't matter because he's giving me great orgasms, but sometimes I really feel like nothing more than a fucktoy. Being a fucktoy when the person loves you is so much better than emotionless sex.

I haven't been sleeping well, because I've been so keyed up about Noah. It finally caught up with me, and I've napped as soon as I got home from work the last few days. When my breasts start aching, I tell myself to not jump to conclusions. It just means my period is about to start. I've been down this road before.

The next day, when my scrambled eggs are unappealing and I'm nauseous at the thought of food, I realize it's time for a pregnancy test. This time I don't tell Noah I'm taking one. After work, I drive to the nearest pharmacy and snicker. Yes, I could've picked one up at work, but there's no way in hell I want one of my coworkers to know what's going on in my life. I slip into the drugstore and pick up my test, along with a gigantic bag of peanut M&M's. I can eat my feelings with peanuts and chocolate if the test is negative.

I know I should probably wait until morning, but the box has three test strips, so if it's negative tonight, I'll just test again when I get up tomorrow. After I follow the instructions, I set it on the counter and set a timer on my phone. I'm so nervous I can't stay in the bathroom and pace around the bedroom. Maybe I should tell Noah I took a test tonight? No, he'd ask to come over, and I don't want to see him. We've been texting good night and good morning, and I'll give him my customary nighttime message and sleep on it.

When the alarm on my phone goes off, I stop pacing, take a deep breath, and mentally prepare myself for whatever the result is. I walk into the bathroom and stare down at the test strip.

It's positive.

I freeze for a moment before blinking a few times to make sure I'm not imagining it. When it still shows the two lines, it sinks in. My heart races, and I wrap my arms around myself and sway a little. Holy fuck, I'm pregnant.

I stumble into the bedroom and sit on the end of my bed, while a massive wave of elation hits me. It worked, it really worked. I flop backwards, giggle, and stare dreamily at the ceiling, imagining how in roughly nine months I'll finally have a baby.

My hands are shaking as I try to text Noah. I'm halfway through typing to tell him I'm pregnant, and I stop. Wait, what am I doing? I'm bursting to share the good news, but not with just anyone. I want that someone to be Noah, but it's possible he won't be happy. Maybe he'll be sad his fucktoy doesn't need him anymore.

I set my phone down on the bed next to me and think about the coming months. This is going to be a lot of doctor appointments and pregnancy symptoms and everything that comes with that. I'm going to be doing all this alone. Staring down at my empty hands, I think about the future, and my ears ring. I shake my head to clear the overwhelming thoughts. Plenty of women do this on their own, and I'm not unique. If they can do it, so can I. In the end, it will be worth it, but fuck, this is going to be hard.

A tiny voice in my head tells me that Noah would probably help me, but he won't be there all the time. I need to learn how to do this myself. If I'm going to have a child depending on me, I don't want to risk getting even more attached while he's only being helpful because I'm pregnant. I never want to hear him explain again how he's not interested in a relationship. Been there, got the message.

The longer I think about it, the more resolved I become. My shoulders relax, and my anxiety settles down. The reason I've been so confused and hurt the last couple of weeks is because I've been wanting him to act loving towards me. The reality is, he's only coming over for the all-you-can-eat sex buffet. Shit, I don't think I can stay friends with Noah. We're not dating, but I'm going to have to break up with him.

I pick up my phone before I change my mind.

The phone barely rings before Noah picks up. His voice is warm and friendly. "Hey, I was just thinking about you."

Shit, he sounds happy. My neck muscles tighten, and I switch the phone to my other ear as I sit up on the edge of the bed again. Squaring my shoulders, I forge ahead. "Noah, we need to talk."

My heart thuds twice while he pauses. The warmth is gone, and he gives a cautious, "What's up?"

Rubbing the back of my neck, I bite my lip and struggle with my words. Why is this so difficult? He's stated multiple times he doesn't want a relationship. Sure, he enjoys my company, and will miss the sex, but it shouldn't hurt his feelings. He'll probably be dating someone new next week. He said he doesn't have problems finding sexual partners when he wants one. Imagining him screwing someone else and calling them his fucktoy creates a burning sensation in my chest, and I want to kick something. Why am I letting this bug me?

Fuck it. I sit up taller and take a deep breath. Keeping a steely resolve in my voice, I state matter-of-factly, "I'm pregnant, and I decided it would be better for me and the baby if I didn't see you anymore."

He peeps out a startled, "What?"

I refuse to let it stop me and continue. "I didn't realize I would feel this way, but it's for the best."

"Wait, Lexi—"

I'm trembling as I cut him off. "Don't worry, I have your email address, and I'll send you picture updates after the baby is born. If I forget, email me."

"But—"

I don't stop talking. "Oh, I'll also let you know when it's born and its name." Each interruption makes me more determined to get everything out.

Adrenaline courses through me, and my thoughts are scattered. I'm dedicated to my current path, but when my throat burns, I know I need to get off the phone because I'm about to break down.

"Lexi, can we talk about this?"

He's sounding flustered, and I hate that I want to cuddle and stroke his back while assuring him I don't mean any of this.

I frown into the phone. "No. I need to focus on myself and the baby."

"But—"

I snap, "Noah, thank you for your service. I'll be in touch."

My heart races, and I hear another faint, "Wait, I need to tell you—" as I hang up.

Tears sting my eyes, and I stare off into space for a moment. Ugh, was this a mistake? I jump when my phone rings. My screen tells me it's Noah, and I hit decline. Nope, sorry...can't talk. If I speak with him right now, I might change my mind, and this is what I need.

A moment later he tries calling again, and my nostrils flare in annoyance. I glare at the phone before sending him to voicemail. Now he's pissing me off. I've been waiting weeks for him to open up to me and do more than fuck me, but he had his chance to talk. He never even told me where he went on his trip. Where did he go? If he cared for me, he would have told me...and those days he didn't contact me and I worried he was in an accident? Fuck him.

Putting my phone on Do Not Disturb, I lie back and close my eyes as tears trickle towards my ears. Well, this sucks. I feel like I might throw up. I wait for a few minutes, uncertain whether I'm going to need to bolt to the bathroom and hurl into the toilet. It's stupid that it's difficult to break up with someone I wasn't even dating. Why did I have to fall in love with him? I can't be around him while I'm hormonal and risk getting more attached.

I drag myself up and wipe the moisture off my cheeks with the edge of my shirt. Fuck this. I refuse to mope for a guy who doesn't love me. I set my jaw, determined to not waste my life mooning over Noah, and change out of my work clothes. Tonight is a good night for comfort food and a movie, so I put on my softest pair of pajamas and mosey into the kitchen. Doing everything I can to avoid looking at the screen on my phone for missed messages, I make a huge mug of hot chocolate and microwave a bag of extra-butter popcorn. Shit, I need something more to eat. A quick search in the fridge reveals sliced ham and cheese. Yeah, this matches my energy level. I roll the meat and cheese together to make tasty little protein sticks and take my bounty to the living room.

Now that I'm pregnant, it's time to tell Kylie what I've been doing with Noah. I'll call her tomorrow and beg forgiveness for avoiding her because I didn't want to explain my crazy. She knows me well enough that I'm sure she thinks something is going on. I'll make my amends and stop being an absent friend.

I'm not hungry, but I force myself to munch on my snacks. Since I dislike cooking, I need to figure out some quick, healthy dinner options. Tonight I've got my protein, and popcorn is a whole grain. We'll pretend that it isn't drenched in fake butter.

Snuggling into the couch, I turn on the TV to hunt for a romantic comedy so I can be mindless and forget the phone call with Noah. After surfing through the movie options and seeing all the love tropes with a happily ever after, I switch the plan to straight comedy. "The Hangover" catches my eye. Perfect. No one falls in love in that movie, from what I can remember. I eat part of my food—enough to satisfy my conscience —and stretch out on the cushions. I grab the blanket off the back of the couch and burrow under it while watching the movie.

As I relax and get warm, I drift off, only to wake briefly when an advertisement auto plays at the end of the movie. I'm exhausted and groggy, so I turn the TV off and can't resist checking my phone. There are two missed calls and several text messages from Noah. I'm too tired to read the messages, so I drop my phone on the floor and fall asleep.

CHAPTER
Eighteen

I'm in a state of shock for two days. I call in sick to work and do nothing but binge watch comedy and horror movies while I try to avoid thinking about Noah. When I can't get off the couch and go to work on the third day, I realize it's time to call in reinforcements. I send Kylie an 'SOS, I need you' text, and she responds she'll be over in an hour.

As I'm cleaning up my condo, I glimpse myself in a mirror. Oh shit, I need a shower. I've been living in the same nightgown for three days and barely left the couch. Kylie will forgive a dirty kitchen, but I need to be clean by the time she gets here. I take a long shower and put on fresh pajamas, feeling more like myself.

I'm downstairs and anxiously chewing on my fingernails when the doorbell rings. When I open the door, I take one look at Kylie and burst into tears. She rushes in and extends her arms for me to fall into. My vision blurs and my throat is scratchy, but her embrace soothes me. She's tall and sturdy, and she's always joking she should have joined a rowing team. I sob into her comforting, broad shoulders while she rubs my back and murmurs words of encouragement. She doesn't even know why I'm crying.

When she can tell I'm cried out, she finally asks, "Which guy needs his legs broken?"

I sniffle while I laugh and step back from her. "His name is Noah, and I'm pregnant."

Her eyes sparkle with anger, and her skin flushes. I can tell she's getting worked up, but before she goes on a tirade, I start to fill her in on what's been happening.

"I kind of decided I wanted a baby and went online to find a guy to get me pregnant. Noah was the chosen one."

I'm pretty certain she wasn't expecting that. She looks taken aback, and the indignation fades. "So what went wrong?"

My heart hurts, and I swallow and sniffle again. "I fell in love with him, and he doesn't love me."

Admitting he doesn't love me is almost my undoing, and she crushes me against her. I rest my head on her shoulder again and enjoy her strength and softness while she pats my back. Everyone needs a friend like Kylie. Even though my nose is stuffy, I can smell her lilac perfume. She's been wearing the scent for so long, whenever I smell it, I think of her. The familiarity soothes me and makes me feel safe.

Her voice is soft and non-judgmental. "I think you need to fill me in on what you've been doing while you've been avoiding my phone calls."

Yeah, it's time for me to tell her the complete story, even though it's going to sound ridiculous. We move to the couch, and I shove my feelings aside so I don't cry the entire time while spilling my guts about Noah. It's difficult to admit my lowest point, but I tell her about the last two days where I was nonfunctional and eating pizza for every meal.

She's all business after I'm done with my story. "Well, Lexi, that ends now." I nod my head and she continues. "You're an incredibly strong woman. You made it through losing Josh, and you don't need Noah...and frankly, if he doesn't want you, he's an idiot."

My smile from her pep talk doesn't reach my eyes, and I glumly respond, "Yeah, I suppose." I don't sound convincing to either of us, but it's a start.

Kylie eyes my messy living room and gets up. "I want you to sit down and rest while I tidy up."

I almost protest, but shrug and snuggle in on the couch. I'm feeling crappy enough, so it's nice to have someone taking care of me.

"Fine, but we've talked about me long enough. What's going on with you?"

While she cleans, she tells me about the new guy she's dating. Whenever she says his name, she practically glows. I can't help feeling a little jealous, but she deserves to find love and I'm genuinely happy for her. She's had a rough life. It's wonderful that she found a guy who treats her right.

When she takes plates and trash to the kitchen, I peek at my phone. There are ten missed text messages from Noah. I frown as I scan through them and they go from pleading with me to sounding indignant that I won't respond. The last one is him saying he won't contact me again.

My mind races. Fuck, what did he want to tell me? I ponder what it might have been, but when I feel myself getting upset, I shake my head. Maybe if it was that important, he should've said it in text so I would know. It's not like I'm going to contact a pissed-off man. Not that it matters anyway, because he doesn't want a relationship.

I'm annoyed at myself for not hearing him out, but I'm not into pointless conversations that will just prolong my hurt. My shoulders slump. This all sucks.

At least Kylie seems to forgive me for avoiding her for so long. If she had brushed me off, I would have been devastated. But she was busy with this new guy and must have understood I had something going on and would talk when I was ready.

When she doesn't return from the kitchen, I venture in there to figure out what she's doing. I find her going through my fridge and tossing out expired foods.

Since she's half in the fridge, reaching towards the back, and her voice is slightly muffled. "Tonight I think we should order something that is NOT pizza, and then I'll swing by tomorrow and we can go to the store and stock up on healthier options."

A flood of affection for her washes over me. I really have an amazing friend. "That sounds good. I need to eat better for the baby."

When I say, "the baby," aloud, my entire body tingles and it really sinks in.

Holy shit, I'm pregnant and alone.

~

Over the next couple of weeks, Kylie checks in on me daily. We go out to dinner a few times, and she takes me shopping to make sure I'm buying healthy groceries and not subsisting on pizza. Things had been going really well with her and the boyfriend, but they ran into a bumpy patch, so she needed a friend to talk to. It's nice to set aside my worries and listen to her for a change.

My days blur together. My hormones are a mess, and morning sickness is a "fun" bonus. It'd be easier to get over Noah if I wasn't pregnant and thinking about him daily while his baby grows inside me. Despite saying he would not contact me again, he still texted me goodnight for a week. I got an odd comfort from them, even though I didn't respond. The night it stopped was the worst night since I told him I couldn't see him. It slashed my heart to pieces, and I sobbed into my pillow for hours. I almost called in sick to work the next day, but I had to keep all the sick days I could in case I needed them later.

I tried to explain it to Kylie, and I'm not sure I did a good job, but abruptly cutting myself off from Noah was almost like going through withdrawal symptoms. He kept me on a roller coaster of highs for days, and I think I got addicted to him. I don't know how to get over him.

On my next day off, I tell Kylie I want to veg in my pajamas all day and be alone. She offers only a mild protest, and I happily settle on the couch with an enormous bowl of buttered popcorn and a movie. I try not to imagine cuddling with Noah while I do. I'm not in the mood for a romance, so I queue up the next season of Stranger Things to watch. The popcorn smells amazing, but as soon as I take a few bites, a knot forms in my stomach and I lose my appetite.

I stare into space and miss the first part of the show. Shit, I need to pull myself together. When I blank out and another few minutes pass, I give up and turn off the TV. What would have happened if I had never told Noah I couldn't see him anymore? I bet I wouldn't be living with 24/7 anxiety. I rub the back of my neck and replay the last conversation with Noah in my head, remembering all the times he tried to interrupt me. What was he going to say? That's been the real problem all this time. I'll never know if he was going to say something that would have changed my mind.

Stretching out on the couch, I wrap my arms around my waist. Then there's the matter of you, my tiny little nugget, that is supposed to have Noah's eyelashes. How badly will it hurt if you do? Or maybe after all those months it won't matter anymore, but how could I not think of him every time I look at you?

When my phone rings, I jump in surprise and then giggle. Shit, I'm really on edge. I glance at the screen and don't recognize the number. Nerves flutter in my belly. What if I answer and it's really Noah? I can always hang up. Fuck it, let's find out.

I sit up and answer. "Hello?" My chest tightens. Shit, I actually hope it's Noah.

It's a woman's voice. "Is this Lexi?"

"Yes…"

"My name is Kristine. Did Noah tell you about me?"

Um…who the fuck is Kristine?

I wrack my brain. Did Noah mention anyone named Kristine? His wife's name was Josie, but I don't remember a Kristine.

"Lexi? Are you there?"

Fuck it, let's pretend I know who she is.

"Oh, sorry. Yes, he mentioned you."

My stomach rolls, and I fight the urge to huff into the phone. This better not be a girlfriend I didn't know about, though that might make me hate him, which would help me get over him.

Kristine gushes, "Ohhh, good. I was so afraid to call you. If he knew I was even doing this, he'd be pissed, but I won't ask you not to tell him. I'll deal with the consequences, but I couldn't just sit here and do nothing."

My thoughts go frantic at her words, and I pick compulsively at a ball of fuzz on my nightgown to calm myself enough to respond. I keep my tone neutral so I don't scare her off. "I don't know what I'm going to do yet since you haven't told me why you called."

"Oh." She giggles, and it sounds nervous. "My wife and I thought it might help if we told you how much we love Noah."

Okay, so not a girlfriend.

When I don't respond, she continues. "Granted, he'd lose his ass if it wasn't attached to his body, but he's a good one. We thought you should know before you potentially make a mistake. He'll make a fabulous father no matter what he thinks, and..."

She trails off, and I need to know. "And what?"

She laughs nervously again. "Rachel and I were hoping to meet you and see if we could be friends so that our kids would know their biological sibling. If we tell Anthony he has a half-sibling out there, he's going to want to meet them."

Ohhhhh, fuck. It clicks into place who Kristine and Rachel are. They're the lesbian couple Noah impregnated. Holy shit. Spots flash in front of my eyes and I shake my head to clear my vision.

This is a lot to take in, but I don't want to scare her off. I don't have any siblings, and this is probably going to be my only child. Having a connection with their family could be good for everyone.

I warm the tone of my voice. "I think I'd like that, but we don't need Noah."

She half snorts. "True, but at least consider talking to him? He's torn to pieces about this and knows he was an idiot. So if you could—"

I cut her off. "He took a trip recently. Was it to see you all?"

If he won't tell me, maybe she will.

"No...but you need to hear about that from him. He's already going to be angry that I butted in this much."

I want to argue with her. If she's already gone this far, she might as well dig her hole deeper. Ugh, but I don't want to push and make her dislike me. This is all sorts of fucked up.

Rubbing the back of my neck, I try to figure out where to go from here. A kaleidoscope of emotions swirls inside my gut, but I don't know which one is strongest. I'm a mix of confused and anxious, but my resolve to hate Noah has a tiny crack.

"Lexi, will you think about it?"

A vision of Noah joining me in bed after he gets off work as we snuggle and talk about our day fills me with an intense longing. I respond thickly, "Yes, I'll consider it."

"Really?" The delight in her voice is clear. "Oh, thank God. He really cares about you."

She continues praising him, but I don't hear her. What am I going to say to him? He stopped talking to me, so I'm going to have to contact him.

What she's saying breaks through to me. "Anyway, I should get going. I'll text you my email address so we can talk more about the future. I know you're busy, and this can wait until after the baby is born."

I murmur, "That's fine," and we both say goodbye before disconnecting.

Tapping my finger against my lips, I reflect on the conversation with Kristine. Should I weigh the pros and cons of calling Noah? The longer I sit in silence, the more I can feel my heartbeat. The strong beats help me decide. I'd love to have Noah at the doctor's appointment when we can hear the baby's heartbeat. If there's a chance that Noah wants to be with me, I'd be foolish not to give him a chance to tell me what he wanted to say before.

My body lightens, and a sense of calmness settles over me. I'm going to do it before I change my mind, and I speed dial him. I don't have time to consider hanging up because he answers immediately with a simple, "Lexi."

It's impossible to read what he's feeling with just one word, but my reaction to his voice is instantaneous. My eyes fill with tears ,and I tremble. Holy fuck, I missed talking to him so damn much, but a spear of hurt knifes me at the same time. I bite down on my bottom lip. I want to see him in person, and I can't handle a long conversation right now since I'm so close to bawling.

I keep my words measured, so he can't tell I'm about to lose it. "Noah, can we talk?"

He pauses for half a second before answering softly. "I'd like that."

When he takes a deep breath, like he's about to say something, I stop him. "Can we do it tomorrow at the coffee shop?"

I need more time to think about this, and in public there's less of a chance I'm going to make a scene if I don't like what he has to say.

"Yes. Does ten work for you?"

I have to work tomorrow, but not until later. "Ten is fine."

"Okay..."

We both sit there in silence. Shit, he needs to know how important this is.

"Noah? When we talk tomorrow, you better make it good. This is your only shot at me listening."

He doesn't respond for a moment. While the silence stretches on, my hands tingle and I flex them while rolling my shoulders to ease the tension. I want to beg him to come over here and hold me while he promises never to fuck up again, but I don't know how he feels. I only have Kristine's word that he cares.

He expels his breath loudly. "I understand. I'll be there at ten."

I almost joke that he better not be late but bite my tongue. Anything I say right now might come out wrong.

"And Lexi?" His voice has an unexpected intensity that tugs at a primal spot deep inside me.

Why can't it be tomorrow already? "Yes, Noah?"

"You won't regret giving me the chance. It'll be good."

My brain freezes, and I manage a tiny, "Oh."

He chuckles at my reaction. "Good night, Lexi. I'll see you tomorrow."

I still don't know how to respond, so I mutter, "Good night, Noah."

He hangs up, and my brain switches back on.

WAIT, he's going to motherfucking say that and not continue?

Gripping the phone, my hands shake, and I fight the urge to call him back and demand to know what he meant, but I'm the one who said we had to wait until tomorrow.

I grumble for a moment and then smile. Well, it serves me right. I rise from the couch and try to distract myself by doing the dishes before bed. I can't help the lightness of my step and the small sliver of hope blossoming in my heart. God, I really love him. Please, please, let this have a happy ending tomorrow.

CHAPTER
Nineteen

I sleep like shit, tossing and turning all night, and finally give up an hour before my alarm goes off. We should have met up last night. I don't know what I was thinking.

I'm yawning as I step into the shower. Dang, I already miss the triple-shot espresso drinks I used to get when I was exhausted. All the advice says a pregnant woman can have moderate caffeine intake, but there is nothing moderate in my needs this morning. One cup of coffee will not be enough.

The shower rouses me, but I'm a bundle of nerves and pace my living room. Is he going to say he loves me? I hate that my brain is even going in that direction because now, if he doesn't, will I get upset? He said I won't regret giving him the chance to talk and it'll be good, but it's possible his idea of what I want to hear differs vastly from what I'm hoping.

If Noah is considering trying to be more than just friends with me, his commitment issues probably require him to take much smaller steps than my mental leap. And yet, I can't stop daydreaming. Walking into the coffee shop and him swooping me backwards in some huge romantic Hollywood kiss while he professes his undying love for me.

I snort as I double check my appearance in the bathroom mirror. It's fine to have a fantasy, but I know the reality is going to be awkward as fuck, and it won't be anywhere near as dramatic.

It's a gorgeous day, so I'm wearing a light pink floral sundress and comfortable yet feminine sandals. Despite the lack of sleep, my eyes are bright and my cheeks match the pink in my dress. I don't need blush today.

Since I've got time to kill, I'm going to walk to the coffee shop and rid myself of this excess energy. I want to be serene and relaxed when he joins me. A small voice deep inside me says I need to be ready for disappointment, but I ignore it. I'm tired of living my life as if the glass is half empty. I'm always waiting for the other shoe to drop and miss out on the joy of anticipation for the good things in life.

I grab my purse and slip my phone and keys into it. When I step outside, the crisp, cool air makes the perfect weather for a stroll. I keep my pace slow and breathe in the smell of freshly cut grass from a nearby lawn. Faint whiffs of exhaust and rubber come from the street, but it's not unpleasant.

Oh yeah, pregnancy has heightened my sense of smell.

I'm a block away from a local bakery, and I swear I can smell the yeasty bread and bagels they baked this morning. My stomach rumbles, and I giggle. I'm going to order an egg sandwich and a strawberry Italian soda when I get there. They have a limited breakfast and lunch menu for fast meals, and I need food before work. I wish it was my day off, but I'm not going to wait until after he says his piece.

There's a spring in my step the closer I get to the shop, and I'm humming a made-up tune. The city recently repaved the street and fixed the sidewalk in front of the coffee shop. I used to have to watch where I stepped so I didn't trip, but the new sidewalk is smoother. It's a little thing, but it adds to the pleasantness of the short walk. The yeasty goodness kicked up my appetite though, so I speed up and my mouth waters at the thought of the egg sandwich. I'll splurge and get it with bacon. Today is a perfect day. Whatever Noah says is going to be the icing on the cake—no, it will be the cake. The beautiful weather is the icing.

I'm less than half a block from the coffee shop when a soft ping from my phone alerts me to a message. Shit, this better not be Noah saying he can't make it. I stop by a tree and fish for my phone. My mood instantly shifts from being one with the world to annoyance, and I tap my foot and narrow my eyes as I swipe the screen. Somehow I know it's Noah. I'm not wrong.

NOAH

> Hey, I'm running 5 minutes late. I'll be there, I promise. Don't leave.

I can't restrain my grin. Holy hell, he warned me he's running late. My mind blips out for a moment before it switches back on. Oh, wow. He's serious about this—us.

Holding in my squeal of happiness, I rock on my heels and re-read the text while I take a couple of steps towards the coffee shop.

I don't have time to react to someone yelling, "Hey!" before a hard jolt to my body pitches me forward. I experience a moment of weightlessness, and then I'm on the ground, on my side, staring at the spinning wheels of a blue bicycle.

That's odd. Why am I lying down?

My hand stings, and I bring it up in front of my face while a few crimson drops run down my palm.

"Hey lady, you okay?"

A teenage kid wearing a bike helmet crouches in front of me. I blink at him before turning my palm towards him.

He screeches, "Oh shit!"

Right before I pass out, I ask him, "Is my baby okay?"

The sirens and lights confuse me, and people are talking to me, but I'm in a weird tunnel and they're at the other end. I can't tell what they're saying. Eventually, I close my eyes, too tired to figure out what's going on. I feel weightless again and crack my eyes open. Oh, someone put me in bed. That was nice of them.

My lids drift shut again.

I feel like I'm moving and it's noisy, so I keep waking up. The first time I'm confused and try to focus on the person next to me, but my stomach rolls and I almost throw up when my vision tilts.

Closing my eyes again helps, and I murmur, "Is the baby okay?"

Someone pats my shoulder, and a soothing voice answers. "We'll be at the hospital shortly, and a doctor will check you out. Just rest."

Some more sleep would be nice, but I was doing something important. I struggle to stay awake. "Is it time for coffee?"

The kind person chuckles. "No coffee right now, I'm afraid. Just rest."

I grumble, "Hospital coffee sucks." The person laughs again as I let my mind turn off.

I wake up several times when I'm poked and prodded by various people, but I always go back to sleep. Eventually, an annoying beep wakes me fully.

Oh shit, I'm in the hospital?

A nurse comes in with a clipboard. When he sees I'm awake, he asks for a bunch of information and fills out some forms. The longer he talks, the more my head clears, and I can tell I'm in the emergency room. Noah is going to think I ditched him. I bolt straight up in panic, and my head about splits in two from the pain.

I glance around frantically. "Where's Noah?"

The guy stops writing and looks at me. "There is a guy in the waiting room. Do you want to allow him back here?"

Some of my tension eases. "Yes, please."

The nurse leaves, and I relax back onto the bed.

A few minutes later, Noah rushes in. As soon as I see him, time slows down, and I burst into tears. He pulls a chair close to the bed, sits down, and grips my hand.

"It's okay, Lexi. I'm here."

He gives my hand little kisses and holds it while I sob. It's been so long since I've seen him, and I've been so fucking miserable these last couple of weeks. I pour all my loneliness and upset into my tears and let loose. He strokes my hand and arm and doesn't speak while I bawl.

The tears finally quiet, and I sniffle. My nose is running, and my eyes are gummy. When I take a few shuddering breaths and sniff again, he moves away long enough to grab some tissues. I take them from him and notice a bandage on the hand he wasn't holding.

What's this? A vision of the crimson drops on my hand and being on the ground comes back to me, and my eyes widen as I stare at Noah.

"A kid on a bicycle hit me." My voice is filled with disbelief and confusion.

He kisses the fingertips of the hand he's holding. "I know. I got there right after they took you in the ambulance. I talked to a couple of people who saw what happened and knew it was you. The kid was fine—just scared."

"Oh."

I guess that explains why he's here, and I'm glad the kid didn't get hurt. I study the bandage on my hand and can tell it wasn't anything major. My hand is sore, and I assume there are probably a couple of stitches under the bandage.

A doctor comes in with a friendly smile. "Hi, I heard you were awake."

She introduces herself, and I sigh in relief. She wouldn't be smiling if something happened to the baby, would she?

Noah stands up, but doesn't release my hand. "I'll give you some privacy and come back in a few minutes."

I'm startled and tug on him. "No, don't go. Stay."

I'm not ready to let him out of my sight yet, plus the doctor won't say anything I don't want Noah to hear.

Taking a deep breath, I address the doctor. "Is the baby okay?"

The doctor's voice is soft. "It seems to be. You aren't far along, but you're going to need to rest for a few days. You slept longer than we expected."

I snort at her comment. "Yeah, I got very little sleep last night."

She smiles at that. "Yes, you've been asking everyone who comes into the room for coffee."

Noah coughs. It sounds suspiciously like he's trying to cover a laugh. I want to punch his arm, but the hand I'd use is the one with the bandage. I'll get him back later.

The doctor explains that the cut on my hand needed stitches, and that as long as I have someone at home to monitor me for a few days, they won't keep me at the hospital. It seems I had a nasty fall, but they examined me because of the baby.

When Noah hears I need someone to watch me, his immediate, "I'll be there," warms my heart. The doctor says she'll get my release started and leaves, so I turn to Noah, uncertain what we're going to do when we leave.

Noah speaks before I get a chance. "Can we stay at my house tonight? I want to show you something."

What would he need to show me at his place? "Um...sure."

My hesitancy comes through my voice, so Noah leans over the bed and kisses me softly. "You won't regret it. I promise."

He sits back down, and I give him a direct look. "And we need to talk."

He nods. "Yes, and we need to talk."

Twenty

As soon as we get to Noah's place, he hovers around me like a mother hen. The hip I landed on is sore, but overall I'm not feeling bad. I didn't hit my head hard, and the small bandage on my hand is the only visible mark I have from the fall. But he's treating me like I'm glass and going to shatter.

I'm bundled on his couch with pillows, a blanket, hot chocolate, and a delicious turkey sandwich. I don't mind being pampered occasionally, so I relax and enjoy the attention. It's been a couple of shitty weeks, and his attitude is a welcome change after thinking he didn't want to be with me. He brings out another blanket and drapes it over the back of the couch. Is this in case I get cold with one?

"Are you comfortable? Do you need anything else? Water...juice?" He gives me a hopeful expression, and I smile into the mug as I take a sip of hot chocolate.

"I'm fine. Just sit with me."

He settles at the other end of the couch and gives me a long look. As he studies me, a tiny wrinkle appears in his forehead, as if he's debating something. My heart pounds at his nearness. I yearn to have his arms around me, but I won't fall into old patterns without clearing the air. I'm also determined that *he* needs to be the one who talks. He wanted me to come here, and he said I wouldn't regret it, but I refuse to smooth this over and make things okay for him.

I did a lot of thinking on the drive from the hospital. I've been through way too much shit, and the accident changed things for me. Everything I've been working towards could have been gone in an instant. I'm still processing what happened, but I'm not interested in half measures from Noah; either he's in or he's out. My stomach muscles tense, and I'm flooded with uncertainty.

Please, God, let him be all in.

I'm still exhausted despite sleeping at the hospital, and the warmth of the blanket and hot chocolate makes me drowsy. If he wants to talk, he better do it soon before I fall asleep. I raise my eyebrows and give him a questioning gaze.

He takes the hint and clears his throat. "I know I need to tell you stuff, but I'm afraid I'm going to fuck it up."

Well, at least he's starting from a place of honesty, but I'm not ready to give an inch yet. I tell him, dryly, "You'll fuck it up more if you don't talk."

Surprise flits across his face before his mouth twists into a wry smile. "Good point."

When he pauses again, I change my mind. I have something I need to know. "Why didn't you reply to me on your trip? Why the radio silence?"

He rakes his fingers through his hair nervously. "I went to visit Josie's parents. They had a shed in their backyard full of stuff they wanted me to go through."

Why in the hell would he be secretive about that?

He continues. "After she died, I just left. I grabbed some clothes and ran. I couldn't deal with our stuff. They offered to help, but I didn't realize they kept it all this time. They're moving and asked me to come."

Snuggling deeper into the blanket, I frown at him. "Why didn't you tell me this?"

He shrugs. "Because I'm a fucking idiot."

I let my displeasure show. I was hoping for a better explanation. He told me where he went, but he didn't tell me why the silence. So far, this isn't going great. Fuck, maybe I should have napped first since I can't tell if being tired is affecting how I'm reacting.

We're both silent for a moment. When he doesn't speak again, a flush of heat runs through me and I get pissed. Fuck this. I set my mug and sandwich plate on the coffee table and pull the blanket off me. I swing my legs to the floor, intending to get up, but he stops me by speaking.

"Where are you going?" he blurts out in a higher-pitched voice than usual.

I glare at him and speak slowly. "I'm going home. You're clearly incapable of opening up to me, and I'm tired of this." My bluster is gone by the end of the brief explanation, and I sigh. "I'm tired of everything."

"Lexi, wait...please. Give me a chance?"

His puppy dog look and beautiful hazel eyes with the long eyelashes melt my heart. Shit, okay. I fold my hands in my lap and angle towards him. "I'm listening."

His words tumble out in a rush. "I told you I was in therapy, and I've worked on communicating better, but I've never cared about anyone this much since losing Josie. I feel like I'm still fucking everything up."

A thrill runs through me when he says he's never cared this much since Josie. Okay, this is getting better. I want to tell him we've been over him potentially fucking it up, but he continues.

"I was an emotional wreck on the trip. Being back there was harder than I expected. I didn't want to burden you with my shit, since I wasn't sure you wanted to be with me. We were just having fun trying to get pregnant. I didn't let myself think beyond that. Then you surprised me that night you made dinner when it seemed like you wanted more."

Yeah, when he told me he didn't want to be a father and that he hoped we could stay friends.

He can tell I'm remembering what he said. "Yeah, I fucked up that night, too."

I give him a tiny nod. It's still not totally better, but at least he's talking.

"I really thought I would be a horrible father."

My heart hurts and I want to call him a moron, but I tamp down my frustrations and keep my voice soft. "Do you still think that?"

He stands up and holds out his hand to me. "Can I show you something?"

I tilt my head to the side and contemplate his offered hand before shrugging and sliding my uninjured palm into his. I might as well see where this is going. He helps me off the couch and guides me down the hall to a room I've never been in before. The door was always closed, like it is now. There's a tingling at the base of my neck, and I'm curious. Am I going to find a secret sex dungeon or a weird collection of creepy dolls once he opens the door?

He puts his hand on the doorknob and pauses. "I'm not my parents. I realized this after you told me you were pregnant and didn't want to talk. My dad wouldn't have given a shit and would have been glad to not have to deal with a baby. I wasn't."

He pushes the door open and turns on the light. I blink and it takes a moment for me to comprehend what I'm seeing. My knees go weak and I turn to him with wide eyes.

Holy fuck.

I'm speechless and frozen in place. The room is a nursery with cream-colored walls and wooden furniture. Everything matches and is obviously new. He put shelves on the walls and a rocking chair next to the crib. All that's missing is decorations and bedding, which are items I'd love to pick out.

My heart thuds in my chest, and I don't know how to respond as I struggle to find the right words. What does this mean? I turn towards him, and my eyes bore into his for several moments until a panicked expression flitters across his handsome features.

He rocks on his heels and babbles. "I'm not my father, and I don't want to be. I was a dumbass, and I should have explained everything. I kept telling myself not to hope for more, but while I was clearing out the storage shed of Josie's things, I kept thinking about how I wished I was home with you." My breath quickens as he continues. "I want to be with you, if you'll give me the chance."

I break eye contact and study the room again, filled with wonder. He did all of this when he didn't even know if I'd talk to him again. It's also pretty early to be decorating a nursery, and I'm touched by his effort and optimism. The only problem is that he still hasn't said what I need to hear.

My voice is quiet. "For how long?"

"What?" he squeaks out, and I want to wrap my arms around him and assure him we can work everything out, but I'm still not sure if we can.

"How long do you want to be with me? Is this a, let's try it out and see if we'll work together situation, or is it more?"

"It—" His voice breaks on the word, and he clears his throat. "It's more."

He reaches for both my hands and entwines his fingers with mine, being careful not to put pressure on my bandage. His touch soothes me, and the wall I built around my heart cracks wide open.

I raise my eyes to his, and he's gazing down at me tenderly. "I love you, Lexi. I want to be with you, and in your life, if you'll have me."

I'm lightheaded at his words, and the tension in my body drains. A rush of joy hits me, and I'm overwhelmed.

He finally said it.

I step in closer and press against him as tears well up behind my eyelids. I do my best to blink them away.

My voice is husky when I speak. "I love you too."

He brings a hand up to cup my face and traces the outline of my lips with his thumb. He lowers his mouth to mine, and his lips are soft, brushing against me. His gentleness is almost my undoing.

Raw hunger pulses through me, and I demand more from him, sliding my tongue inside his mouth and tasting him deeply. As our tongues twine, my body zings alive and desire blossoms in my core. It's been weeks since I've felt his skin against mine, and knowing he loves me changes everything.

He takes control of the kiss, blinding me with passion as he walks me backwards until the length of my body is against the wall. His mouth possesses me, and every thought drains from my head except the desire to get my hands on his naked body and the craving for his cock inside me.

When I run my uninjured hand down his chest and attempt to undo his jeans, he pulls back. "We can't do this. You need to rest."

I move my hand lower and brush against his hardness. "No, I need you to be inside me."

He groans as I rub him, and after a moment, he grabs my wrists and gently pins them to the wall.

I arch against him, not wanting to break contact. "Please, Noah?"

My plea cracks his willpower and desire burns in his eyes. "Are you sure?"

I give him my most seductive voice. "Make love to me, Noah. Claim me again."

The corners of his mouth tug up, and he leans in and kisses my neck before whispering in my ear. "I'm going to do all the work, and you're going to take the pleasure."

"Yes," I moan as he licks the sensitive skin along my collarbone and shivers of delight tickle my spine.

This sounds perfect to me.

"And you know what else?" He trails fervent kisses up to my ear and nibbles on my earlobe.

My body buzzes, and it's hard to think. "Mmm, what?"

"Just because you're pregnant doesn't mean I'm going to stop breeding you. I'm going to fill you so full of my cum you're going to be dripping."

My brain freezes at his words, and I suck in my breath in surprise. Within a moment, my senses turn back on with a whoosh. My nipples harden and ache while my pussy hums with neediness.

Oh hell, yes.

As Noah sweeps me up into his arms and carries me to his bedroom, my yearning for him drains all thoughts of anything but this moment from my mind. He sets me down gently beside the bed and applies pressure on my shoulders until I'm sitting on the edge. Warmth radiates from my belly as he carefully pulls my sundress over my head to remove it, avoiding jostling my bandaged hand. Every movement of his is tender and loving as he helps me take off my strapless bra. When he tugs on my panties, I lift my ass off the bed, and he slides them from under me and down my legs. Each clothing item gets tossed in a pile on the floor.

Once I'm naked, he steps back and examines me with hooded eyes blazing with lust. "Fuck, you're gorgeous."

I peep, "Oh," as a tingling sensation zips straight to my pussy.

Unexpected shyness makes it impossible to look at him, and I study the carpet. I assumed he would toss me on the bed and ravage me, but this soft, loving approach makes me ache with longing. He's treated me like this before, but his actions have more meaning now that I know he really loves me.

His voice is gruff. "Lexi, look at me."

I lift my eyes to his, and his pupils darken with desire.

I'm spellbound as he removes his shirt and keeps talking. "It's been days since I've come. Do you know what that means?"

I focus on the hardness in his jeans, imagining his balls full and ready to burst. I tremble from arousal and my already hard nipples stiffen further as my heart rate speeds up. This is so fucking hot. I still want him to fill me up with cum. I'm not sure why I thought that my breeding kink would go away once I was pregnant, but I want his seed even more now.

The surprising thing is I don't want his cum only in my pussy. I want him to cover me with it and fill every hole. I want him to glaze my breasts as I watch him lose himself in ecstasy. My body craves Noah, and I've never felt this way with any other guy.

He pauses with his jeans halfway undone. Oh shit, he's waiting for an answer.

I sound breathy when I reply. "It means you're going to have a lot of cum for me."

Humor touches his lips, and his eyes sparkle. "Yes. I'm going to pump you so full it's going to be dripping out of you for days. But do you want to know what's different about tonight?"

I nod and stay quiet as he shoves his pants down, freeing his thick cock, and steps out of them. Fuuuuck, why did I think I could live without him? He's all I've wanted for months now.

He moves close enough to use a finger under my chin to tip my head up. "Tonight, my fertile goddess, you won't have to beg for it. You're going to have to take it."

I close my eyes and moan, "Yes," as he crushes his body to mine, forcing me backwards as he covers me. Our lips meet in a wet, hot slide as I wrap my legs around him. His cock is trapped between us, his hardness poking into my stomach. He tugs me up further onto the bed until we're in the middle. I never want to let him go, and he rains kisses on me as I melt into a puddle of delight.

When I try to run my hands between us to rub his cock, he growls and captures my wrists, securing them above my head. "No touching."

Ugh, right. I buck against him, trying to get his cock closer to my pussy. He needs to be inside me right now. If he doesn't fuck me soon, I'm going to beg, whether or not he wants me to.

He lets go of my wrists, and his mouth wanders from mine, tracing the contours of my throat. I loosen my legs so he can move down my body easier. I learn my breasts are extra sensitive when his mouth gets to them. He cups the underside of one to hold it while he licks and sucks at the tip. His thumb and forefinger tease the taut bud on the other breast, and I gasp from the spike of pleasure.

I can't hold back any longer. I groan, "God, Noah, please fuck me."

He murmurs, "Soon," against my breast and continues to swirl his tongue around my nipple. A hand slips between my thighs. He brushes my damp curls before his fingers part my wet folds, seeking my slippery, aching clit. As he caresses the swollen nub, I shiver from ecstasy and rock my hips against his hand.

I mewl, "Ohhhh, god," as my body tightens and electricity builds in my core. His mouth on my breast while he's rubbing me is more than I can handle. I'm racing towards my climax, and I run the fingers of my uninjured hand through his hair and grab a fistful, tugging on it. I moan when he increases the suction on my nipple before letting it pop out of his mouth.

When he looks up at me, I whimper, "Noah, please fuck me. I need you."

He smiles and moves to kiss me deeply, and I sigh into his mouth as he works my clit faster. Oh fuck. I buck against his hand and almost come, but he removes his fingers at the last second. I moan from the denied orgasm, but it turns into a squeal of delight as he plunges his cock into me with one powerful stroke.

"Oh my god," I cry, and our hips move together as we rock back and forth.

Tension coils low in my belly as each hard thrust sends me reeling. I'm buzzing with pleasure, and I'm going to climax any second now.

I chant, "Fuck me, fuck me," as he's ruthless, plowing into me and driving deep.

I'm beyond any reasonable thought, and my body convulses around him, so close to coming, as my thighs quiver. He drills into me. Each whack against my pussy slams his headboard against the wall. The room is a chorus of thuds combined with our gasps and moans.

I'm desperate and so close to coming it's almost painful. I whimper, "Oh, god I want to come," and he groans and fucks me harder. When he brings one hand between us and rubs my clit in tight, fast circles, it pushes me over the edge. I scream his name, bucking against him as energy rips through my entire body. Ripples of pleasure run the length of my body as he jackhammers into me, seeking release.

He pants, "Do you want me to come in you?"

"Yes," I whimper, barely coherent.

He continues to fuck me vigorously. "You're meant for this, Lexi. I can't wait until you swell with my baby."

His words make my head spin, and I can't catch my breath.

"I'm going to come in you and mark you as my own."

Oh, fuck. I don't respond with words and can only moan.

He gives a few sharp prods and demands, "Ask me to breed you."

I'm still shuddering from the aftershocks of my orgasm and rush out a jumble of words. "Breed me please...fill me with your seed until I'm so full it streams out of me...give me everything you've got."

He breathes out a, "Yesss," as his cock pulses and he explodes.

He gives a roar of pleasure as he shoots ropes of warm cum deep inside me. His eruption is violent, leaving him gasping as his body trembles. He pumps into me several times until he's finished and then collapses and melts into my embrace.

I'm in a daze as he relaxes against me and murmurs softly. "I love you, Lexi."

I think I say it back to him, but I'm floating in a sea of contentment after letting go of the stress from the emotional rollercoaster I've been on.

At some point, he pulls out and snuggles next to me as my eyelids droop. I'm so out of it from exhaustion that everything has a dreamy quality.

"Lexi, are you okay?"

The worry in his voice wakes me up enough to mumble, "Mmm...is good...make me breakfast in the morning."

He pulls me closer to him and kisses my shoulder. "I will."

I mumble, "Good," and that's the last thing I remember.

When I wake up, I'm facing the nightstand. My brain is so fuzzy it takes a moment for me to realize what I'm looking at. There's a glass of water on the nightstand with a small silver bell next to it. A sticky note attached to the bell says, "Ring me when you wake up."

Oh, that's sweet. My heart gives a few strong, happy beats, and I smile as I lean up on my elbow and take a sip of water. My bandaged hand twinges from pain, and I wince. It feels worse this morning, so it's good I convinced him to make love to me last night. But even the pain can't diminish the delight welling up inside me.

He loves me.

I ring the bell and snuggle back into bed. What's up with the bell? Couldn't I have called or texted him? It seems old-fashioned but oddly decadent, like I'm ringing for room service. It doesn't take long before I hear him whistling an unidentifiable tune that gets louder the closer he gets to the bedroom.

He comes in carrying a tray with a mound of food. "Breakfast, as you requested."

"I requested breakfast?"

I don't remember it, and I'm confused as he sets up the tray in the middle of the bed next to me. I prop myself up on the pillows so I'm sitting up and snag a piece of bacon to munch on.

Noah climbs onto the bed on the other side of the tray and eats a strip of bacon as well. "Yep. You called me a horny bastard and demanded breakfast."

I stare at him for a moment, uncertain if he's joking. When he can't keep a straight face, I take a decorative pillow that never found its way to the floor and smack him with it.

He yips, "Hey!" and puts an arm over the tray of food, pretending he's trying to protect it. "Don't ruin the peace offering I made."

I nudge his arm away. "Back off the bacon if you want to keep all your limbs."

He laughs. "Fair enough." Noah leans against the headboard and watches me nibble on more bacon and a buttermilk biscuit with jam.

I'm a little self-conscious with him watching me like a hawk as I eat, but I see the worry in his eyes so I don't tell at him to stop. The dull pain in my hand is making me a little grumpy, but I don't want to take it out on him. I'm curious about what he wants to do today.

"So, what's the plan?" I wave a piece of bacon at him as I ask.

"I was thinking you could stay with me and rest until your hand is better, and then we could go out on some proper dates. This might seem backwards, but there's a lot we don't know about each other."

When he stops talking, his face has a pink tint, and he's staring at the tray of food. I blink at him as my heart flutters. Jesus, can he get any more perfect? I take another bite of bacon and enjoy the satisfying crunch.

After I chew and swallow, I flash him a cheeky grin. "I was asking what the plan was for today, but your idea sounds better."

He reaches over, and his fingers encircle the wrist of the hand holding the piece of bacon. He pulls my hand towards him and kisses the back of it.

He keeps his eyes trained on me, and his breath is a warm puff against my skin when he says, "Good."

I wink playfully at him a second before he takes a chomp on MY bacon.

"Hey!" I yank my hand back with a laugh.

His shoulders shake as he picks up a biscuit. Yep, he's cute and he knows it. A sense of calmness envelopes my mind the longer I watch him.

"Hey, Noah?"

He pauses with the biscuit halfway to his mouth. "Yes?"

"Since I'm supposed to rest, I think it's only fitting that you call me 'My Goddess' today and wait on me."

He flashes me a wide smile. "I wouldn't have it any other way, My Goddess."

My body feels weightless and tingly from joy. I want to savor this moment.

He's right. We don't know everything about each other. But when I look at him, I see my future. We're going to have the rest of our lives to explore and learn together because somehow I know we're going to get married.

Epilogue

My hand trembles as I look at myself in the mirror and adjust the veil over my face. I smooth the white, silky fabric of my dress over my enormous belly. Yeah, I'm so going to be waddling down the aisle, but I don't care when Noah is at the other end. I'm eight months pregnant, but when Noah proposed two months ago, I knew I didn't want to wait until the little one arrived. We planned a simple backyard wedding. A few close friends and family are outside waiting for me.

Someone knocks on the door. My "Come in" reveals Kylie.

She's cheery, and her voice is high pitched from excitement. "Hey, everyone is ready."

I sent her out to make sure the marriage officiant was here. Knowing it's time to start has the butterflies in residence in my stomach swirling faster.

I look at her in the mirror. "Am I crazy?"

She pats her newly swelling baby bump that's mostly hidden under her loose, burgundy dress. "No more than I am."

I'm ecstatic our kids will be close in age, if a little apprehensive for her, since she admitted she was sloppy with her birth control on purpose. She got baby fever when I got pregnant. The guy she's dating is crazy for her, but he thinks it was an accident. She doesn't know how he'll react if he finds out she got pregnant on purpose.

He's a really great guy, so I hope it works out for her. Whatever happens, I'll be there for her if she needs me. But she and I agreed that today is only for optimism. Future worries have no place at a wedding.

I avoided thinking of Josh all morning, but as I prepare to leave the room, it's impossible not to compare my life now to how it was before. Memories flood over me. Josh and I had a huge church wedding, and I'm glad I didn't want that again. No matter the location, I'm still pledging my heart to someone else. It's been a long journey to this point, and several crappy years. My vision blurs with tears, and I tremble so much I have to sit on the edge of the bed.

Kylie rushes over to me. "Are you okay?"

Her voice holds concern, and I give her a wobbly smile. "If there is a heaven and Josh is up there, do you think he approves of me marrying again?"

"Oh, Lexi."

She sighs, sits on the bed, and puts her arm around me.

"You know, if he's watching over you, he's rooting for you and Noah. You deserve happiness, and you're lucky enough to have found love twice. Josh wouldn't have wanted you to be alone, and Noah is awesome."

Yeah, Noah is amazing. My heart warms as I think about him, and I blink away my tears before they fall and ruin my makeup. I didn't know I'd ever be able to love again after losing Josh, but I found out my love isn't finite. At some point, I realized I could be passionately in love with Noah without taking from anything I'd had with Josh. It just meant I had a large capacity to love.

I tried to explain it to Kylie once, and she mostly grasped it once she likened it to polyamory and the ability to be in love with more than one person at the same time. Yeah, it's not really the same, but similar enough, so I went with it.

Kylie rubs my arm, and we sit in silence for a few minutes. Her warmth and closeness help the trembling die down.

When my moment of apprehension is gone, she gives me a cute grin. "Are you ready?"

I smile back at her as my heart leaps with joy. "Yep, let's do this."

~

Noah and I stand facing each other through the wedding ceremony. Love pours out of him as he holds my gaze and recites our vows. Everything else blurs together, but the adoration and complete happiness radiating from him tells me he loves me with a deep, abiding passion.

When we exchange rings and link our hands together, a hummingbird zips between us. It only visits us for a moment, barely time to react before it's gone. Noah jerks in surprise but keeps his hands in mine. I laugh, delighted, as my heart drums loudly in my ears. The hummingbird is a message to me that the universe approves of our marriage. My step is light as the ceremony ends, and I'm euphoric as we start our reception celebration.

Later that night, after a long evening of dancing and eating rich food and cake, I dream of my future with Noah and our daughter. When I wake up in his arms, I snuggle against him in total peace.

I thought I only wanted a baby, but the universe knew I needed Noah, too. I found my happily ever after.

The End
Want more sexiness?
Sign up for my newsletter for bonus scenes from Noah's point of view,
including the moment he realizes he loves her.
https://books.april-cross.com/lexi

Hey, here's the working blurb for Claiming Kylie. I'm sure Kylie and Shane won't do exactly what I want them to. My characters never do.

Follow my author profile at your favorite retailer to get notified of my releases or join my newsletter if you want to keep up with my story progress.

One lie can almost ruin your life...

Shane

I wasn't looking for love, but when Kylie walked through the door at a BDSM play party, her confidence and the twinkle of defiance in her eyes drew me in. I wanted to see if I could bring her to her knees. I expected a little sexy fun, but instead got a woman who challenged my beliefs about everything I thought I wanted. I fell hard and fast, and when she accidentally got pregnant, I was all in, ready to do everything in my power to build a family with her.

Then I discovered her lie. I can't be with a woman who would do what she did, but I'm going to fight for my baby with everything it takes.

Kylie

As hot as Shane was, I knew from the beginning that he wanted to keep things casual. This dirty talking, wonderful dom thrilled me in and out of the bedroom, but I knew it wasn't for keeps. And when I accidentally got knocked up, I didn't know how he'd react. But instead of being disappointed, he stepped up, ready to start a life with me.

And it was magical—at least until he discovered the lie I'd told my best friend, Lexi. It was a little white lie—one intended to keep her from getting hurt. After all, she was doing everything she could to get pregnant, and it had happened to me when I wasn't even trying.

Now Shane is ignoring my calls and he's threatening to get lawyers involved. And the worst part? I never knew how hard I'd fallen for him until he was no longer an option.

I'd do anything to win him back, to build that magical life with him.

About April Cross

I write erotic romances that are ghost pepper spicy romance, but are mainly just an excuse to write a ton of sex—preferably with a hint of BDSM power play.

I also write erotica as Lacey Cross and like to focus on freeuse, wife sharing, and BDSM erotic shorts. I'm all about the women I write experiencing as much pleasure as possible.

Website: https://www.april-cross.com/

If you like short and hot wife sharing or freeuse stories, check out my erotica books.

Lacey's books: https://lacey-cross.com/

goodreads.com/aprilcross

bookbub.com/authors/april-cross

facebook.com/aprilcrossauthor

Acknowledgments

Mating Lexi is my first solo novel. It'll never be perfect, but I'm really proud of my first attempt. With my longer stories, I usually say it takes a village to help me release it, and this one is no different.

Wordcat - Thank you a ton for all your advice and editing when I started this story a year and a half ago. I'm a better writer now, so I know back then you had your work cut out for you when helping me. Some of your comments shaped the story, and this book wouldn't be the same without your input.

Adam - Your editing made this book better after I blundered my way through changes from the beta reader's suggestions. Also, thank you for waiting patiently for several months while I battled with my fear of failure. I really appreciate the support and the help.

Chloe - Thanks for finding a few really amusing mistakes. You always make me laugh.

My beta readers · Thank you for your feedback. You found some excellent things that I needed to adjust, and the book is better after your input.

A huge thank you to **all my readers** who were with me on this journey while I wrote Mating Lexi in serial form before taking it to ebook. For the longest time, I thought I was only good at writing short erotica. Your comments and encouragement helped me see I can write longer stories and not limit myself.